Outside the office, it seemed darker in the basement than it had before I realized that that was because someone had closed the door at the top. The someone was standing just inside the closed door, pointing a gun at me. He flicked on the light. He was a tall, thin man with a narrow, bloodless face. Beside him was a sweet little roly-poly woman of about fifty with silver-white hair.

"Church out already?" I asked.

"See if he's got a gun," the woman said. Her voice didn't sound sweet.

A KILLING IN KANSAS

Jeffrey Tharp

FAWCETT GOLD MEDAL • NEW YORK

A Fawcett Gold Medal Book
Published by Ballantine Books
Copyright © 1991 by James Girard

Library of Congress Catalog Card Number: 91-91901

ISBN 0-449-14730-4

Manufactured in the United States of America

First Edition: August 1991

Why trouble him now who sees and hears
No more than what his innocence requires,
And therefore to no other height aspires
Than one at which he neither quails nor tires?
He may do more by seeing what he sees
Than others eager for iniquities. . . .

Edward Arlington Robinson,
The Man Against the Sky

CHAPTER
ONE

━━━━━━━

I was feeling good. The hot day, one in a long string of hot July days in the southeast Kansas coal mine country, had turned cool as a wind blowing in from the north brought banks of clouds, lowering the temperature so fast I could feel it drop, driving with one arm out the window, alone on the old highway from Independence to Elk Rapids, the lights on the interstate, running parallel a half mile away, blinking on as the dusk gave way to dark.

Rain was coming; I could smell it, and the smell gave me a fierce pleasure. In weeks just past, how many times had I opened the windows of my apartment at night, hoping just for a breeze, something to cool the stale air inside and let me sleep? Now the rain was coming, and I was racing it home, thinking of bed after a fruitless day spent chasing down a burglary suspect's alibi over in Montgomery County. I swallowed the wind that whipped through the windows of the old Celica as I goosed it through the curves and dips that wound around and through the wooded hills and gullies around Elk Rapids, the land that was too rugged to farm but that no longer offered up the coal that had once made the town prosperous, so that it had been left to run wild, a strip of waterproof prairie jungle surrounding one of the larger islands where people lived.

Soundless lightning flickered behind the clouds to the north, making the country music on the radio crackle. I fiddled with the dial, finding a station somewhere far away playing the kind of music I'd grown up with, Wilson Pickett chanting brokenly about the midnight hour, and I whooped and stomped the gas, riding the center line through the tight curves, roaring over the sudden hilltops and into the dark little valleys, singing loudly into the wind along with the crackling radio, just singing nonsense in the parts where I couldn't remember the words.

I shot through a long, straight stretch past a ghostly roadside community—a boarded-up gas station; a row of a half-dozen rental cabins, the motel sign only a rusted metal outline against the sky; an old railroad-car diner with broken windows—and then I rose over the top of a small hill and found myself aimed directly at a pickup truck that was parked half on the road and half off, one of its dim taillights blinking erratically, as if from a loose connection.

I hit the brake and the tires screamed and jerked on the patched concrete, the Celica drifting off center as it came to a stop a couple of yards from the truck.

There was a slender black man with a short gray beard leaning against the truck's front fender, staring across the road. As I came to a stop, he straightened up, as if he'd only just noticed my headlights bearing down on him, and took a belated step out onto the roadway, then stopped and peered into my lights, trying to see around them, to see who I was. On the other side of the road, the place where he'd been looking, was a big white car—a new Chrysler, it looked like—wedged nose-first into the ditch, its tail sticking high in the air.

I backed up and pulled in behind the truck, then reached in the back for my flashlight. Heavy drops of cold water began slapping the pavement as I got out. The rain was in no particular hurry, and the occasional splashes felt good on my arms and neck. I hoped this would be nothing, a fender bender, and I could call it in to the sheriff and head on home, though I wouldn't beat the rain now. A couple of the big drops ran down the black man's face, like tears. I suppose my own face looked the same to him.

"Oh, man," he said as I came near. "Shit, man. I think they dead. Somebody got thrown out, I think. I was going over to look, but . . . I got to get my breath. I'm just . . . I'm goin' over to look in a minute."

I took out my wallet and showed him my badge. He looked at it with a mix of relief and suspicion that I'd seen often enough before, and then gave a sigh and nodded back the direction I'd come from.

"I come over the hill," he said, "and the car was comin' right at me, on the wrong side of the road. I headed for this side and I heard him crunch into the ditch on the other side. Sounded like he hit real hard. Don't know how fast he was goin'. Scared the shit out of me. I ain't seen nothin' more nor heard nothin' from over there since I got out. They must be dead." He shook his head, looking queasy.

"Tell you what I want you to do," I said. "You got a flashlight?"

"Say what?"

"A flashlight. You got a flashlight?"

"Uh . . . yeah. In my truck. Yeah, I got a flashlight."

"Well, you go get it and you stand back up the road, on top of that hill, and head off any traffic that comes along. I'll go take a look at the car. Okay?"

I wasn't sure he'd been listening, but he said, "Oh, yeah, sure, man. No problem. I can do that. I'll get my flashlight. Yeah, that's a good idea, man."

"Maybe even save somebody's life," I said.

"Yeah, right. I'll do it." But he didn't move. He kept glancing beyond me at the opposite ditch.

"I'll go check on the people in the car," I repeated.

He nodded, licked his lips, and turned toward his truck. I turned on my flashlight and walked across the road. The rain had turned into mist, blown by the wind, so that I had to turn my head to the side and blink as I peered at the car. The left front fender was buried in the soft earth at the bottom of the ditch and I couldn't see into the driver's side. The passenger door on the other side stood open, but there was no light on inside the car. My flashlight picked out a woman in tight yellow slacks and a white midriff blouse, lying facedown on the opposite slope of the ditch, her arms in a kind of circle above her head. She might have been thrown clear, but it looked more as if she'd opened the door herself, gotten out, then lain down and gone to sleep in the grass. I went down the steep slope at the rear of the car, digging my heels into the earth, and bent over and shone the flashlight on her face. She was breathing evenly, her eyes closed. I saw no marks or blood, nothing that looked broken. Her face was wet from the rain, as relaxed and sweet as a sleeping child's face. I looked at her for a moment longer, and then turned the flashlight on the open door of the car.

There was a man lying on his side in nearly a fetal position in the front seat, his head bent back, staring at me. There was a dark slash of blood on his forehead. I stepped closer and put the light on his face, making him blink. I recognized him. His name was Rob Lucas. I'd talked to him briefly, just a week before, the night William Elmore's body had been found, over on Circle Street, the rich part of town. Lucas had found the body; he lived two doors away from Elmore. But I would have recognized him anyway, because his face was on signs and posters all over town—the square, even jaw, the heavy eyebrows, the swatch of dark hair. The only thing unfamiliar was his eyes. When he opened them to look at me again, they were dull with pain, or perhaps fear, not bright with confidence and determination, the way they looked on the posters.

"How badly are you hurt?" I asked him.

"I . . . I don't know. I'm afraid to move. The steering wheel got me in the stomach." He spoke tightly at first, as

4

though unsure he'd be able to do so without pain, but as he talked his voice loosened up. He slurred his words slightly, but I smelled no liquor on his breath. Concussion, maybe, I thought, but his pupils were the same size, undilated. "I think maybe I cut my head," he said.

"Yeah, there's a little blood. Doesn't look too serious. How's your midsection feel? Is there a lot of pain?"

His gaze turned inward, as though he had to check it out, and then his eyes widened slightly and he shook his head. "Not really," he said. He began to unfold his body cautiously, pushing himself up into a sitting position with one arm.

"Easy," I said.

"I think I'm all right. Just a . . . just a bruise, I think. Yeah. I think I'm all right." He sounded amazed. His eyes brightened a little, although there was still something slack in them.

"How fast were you going?" I asked.

"Not fast, really. I . . . the truck just startled me. It appeared so quickly."

"He said you were on his side of the road."

Lucas looked at me more closely, frowning a little.

"I know you," he said. "You're a cop."

"We met last week," I said.

He nodded. "Oh, yeah," he said. "That's all a jumble in my mind. Seemed like I was asked the same things a hundred times. It was all a madhouse. I'd never seen a body before. Outside a funeral home, I mean." His voice ran down and his eyes drifted away from me, as though something else had caught his attention, then he looked back at me again. "Listen, officer," he said. "I'm sorry I don't remember your name. . . ."

"Branch. Johnny Branch."

"Lieutenant, isn't it? Lieutenant Branch. I remember now. Listen, can't we . . . just sort of forget this? I mean, no one's really hurt. I'll worry about the car."

"What about the lady?"

He leaned forward slightly and looked past me, then said something indistinct under his breath and leaned back again and gave me a sheepish grin. "I thought she left," he said. "I heard the door open after we stopped, and she got out."

"She did. She didn't get very far."

He gave a soft snort of laughter. "Probably passed out," he said.

"Been drinking?"

He shook his head. "Not me," he said. "I was driving."

"She's not a close friend, I take it."

He shrugged. "No. Just a girl Dexter Gennaro introduced me to."

"You a friend of Dexter?" Dexter Gennaro owned a big truck stop complex out on the interstate, with a motel, a pretty good coffee shop, and a private supper club, plus showers and game rooms and a barber shop and laundry for the truckers. A lot of highway patrolmen and sheriff's deputies ate breakfast there every morning, and some of the city cops hung out at the supper club in the evenings. Gennaro was a big man in the Elk Rapids Chamber of Commerce, but most of his friends, as far as I could tell, were guys his own age—Lucas's father's generation.

Lucas held up two fingers, close together. "We're like that," he said. He smiled, but it didn't seem a very happy smile.

"Sit tight," I said. "I'll see if she's come around yet."

He shrugged. "Where am I gonna go, in the rain?" He sounded lost. He leaned his head back and closed his eyes.

The woman was awake now, looking dazed. She had turned over on her back and raised herself onto one elbow. Her short blouse was transparent with rain water and bunched up under her breasts, which were barely encased by a narrow pink bra. She no longer looked innocent and childlike. There were bags under both eyes, and a swatch of her orangy, dyed hair was plastered over one of them.

6

"How you doing?" I asked her.

"I'm dying," she said. "I'm fucking dying." She looked up at me and brushed the hair way, but seemed to have trouble focusing and finally gave up.

I knelt and put a hand under her shoulder. "Let's try to get up," I said.

She shook her head slowly, with what seemed a great effort. Her eyes rolled up a little and I thought for a moment she was going to pass out again, but she didn't. I didn't think she was hurt, but I didn't smell anything on her breath, either.

"I can't," she said. "I'm dying."

"I don't think so," I said. "Come on."

"I've got a pain right here," she said, putting one hand flat on the skin of her stomach.

"Me, too," I said. "Give it a try."

She stuck out her tongue at me, but then took hold of my arm and gave a sudden lunge, getting her legs under her and standing unsteadily, like a colt learning to walk.

"I'm gonna sue the son of a bitch," she said. "Coulda been killed." She tried to take a step and her foot slipped on the wet grass. I caught her and then kept an arm around her, helping her up the slope. She walked by herself on the blacktop, but shakily. The black guy had put on a transparent rain slicker and was standing up the road on the hilltop, looking miserable and bored. He glanced around at us but didn't say anything. I put the woman in the backseat of my car and got a blanket out of the trunk and handed it to her.

"If you have to puke, try to keep it on the blanket," I said.

She closed her eyes and flipped me the finger, but only halfheartedly, a reflex.

I went back to the Chrysler. It was raining more steadily now and wasn't as pleasant as before; the ditch was getting slippery. Lucas was sitting with his legs outside the car, hunched over. The glove compartment was open, and as I approached he shoved something into it. I reached in and

7

grabbed it before he could close it. It was a tubular plastic medicine bottle with no label. Inside were a couple of long white capsules.

"Those are prescription," he said. "I get bad headaches." He was hunched over, shivering. He looked like he was in worse shape than before, maybe in shock.

"What about the lady?" I asked. "She get headaches, too?"

"Cramps," he said weakly. Suddenly he got up and lurched past me, landing on his knees in the wet grass. Holding his stomach tight with both arms, he vomited loudly. It seemed like it took forever. I stood in the rain, trying to remember the good feeling I'd had fifteen minutes before, driving by myself. It was gone.

"I'll radio this in," I said when he'd finished. "They'll send a wrecker for the car. You want me to take you to the hospital, or you want to wait for a paramedic?"

"Christ, no. I want to go home. I want you to take me home." His eyes were closed and he looked exhausted and scared, like a kid, though I guessed he was in his mid-thirties. In that moment, he reminded me a little bit of Eddie Skubitz, the kid who'd been charged in the Elmore killing, although Eddie was a lot smaller, a lot younger, a lot more scared.

"I don't know," I said. "You might really be hurt."

"I'm okay," he said. "I can tell. Just bruises. I was just scared before." He opened his eyes wider and gave me a look of pain that seemed to belie his words. "You know who I am," he said. It was a plea, not a threat.

"What about the lady?" I asked.

"Her too. Bring her too. I'll take responsibility."

I thought about it and then shrugged. "Okay," I said. "I'll take you home. Just remember it was your idea."

I got an arm around him and helped him up the slope, putting him in the front seat. The woman was on her side in the back, snoring, the blanket wrapped around her. He didn't look at her. I flipped on the two-way and told the dispatcher what had happened and where, giving it as a 10–47, not a 10–48. Noninjury. He said he'd relay it to the sheriff's office.

I went back to the Chrysler one more time, for the woman's purse. I found it on the floor in the front. I also pocketed the medicine bottle from the glove compartment. I went back up to my car and tossed the purse on the seat beside the woman, then went to the black man and told him, "Nobody was hurt much. I'm taking them home. The sheriff's department'll send someone to pull the car out. Since the vehicles didn't actually collide, I doubt you'll need to fill out a report, even for the insurance. Far as I'm concerned, you can split. Thanks for the help."

He shrugged, turning off his flashlight. "That's that guy Lucas, isn't it?" he asked. "The one that's running for Congress?"

"Not Congress," I said. "Just the state legislature." I studied his face for a moment, then added, "There's nothing to be made out of this."

He gave a little laugh. "Shit," he said. "I ain't gonna fuck with him. I got my own troubles." As I started to turn away, he said, "Listen, you know I was scared to go over to that car. You knew that."

I nodded.

"Everybody's scared of somethin'," he said. "Nothin' to be ashamed of."

"You talking about me?" I asked, feeling a touch of anger. "You think there's something I'm scared of?"

He put up a hand like a stop sign, his expression blank. "How would I know that, man? I'm just talkin' 'bout myself, that's all."

I nodded, but I didn't really think I'd taken his meaning wrong. Driving to the Lucas home, I wondered what it was the black man had thought he'd seen in my eyes.

CHAPTER
TWO

Lucas's sister had straight black hair, cut short like a rock singer's, wide blue eyes, a small mouth. She was tall—nearly as tall as her brother—and had the slender body of a model. She wore a bright red headband around the dark hair. She gave me a guarded smile through the chained opening in the door, as though she recognized me, but couldn't remember where from.

"Miss Lucas?"

"Yes."

"I'm Lieutenant Branch, Elk Rapids police."

"Yes, I remember. The murder." Her voice was bright, friendly. She might have been talking about a party we'd both attended. She closed the door to unhook the chain, and then opened it wider. She was wearing a pink skintight workout outfit of some thin, slick material—silk, maybe.

"What can I do for you?" she asked.

"I've got your brother out in the car. He's had an accident. Nothing serious, but the car was disabled."

Her hand tightened on the door, and she drew a sharp breath. "Rob? He's not hurt?"

"Just scratches and bruises. He . . . dozed off on the way here. Also the woman he was with. She's in the backseat."

Her lip curled slightly, but then she blanked her features and said, "I'll help you with them."

It had stopped raining, but there was water dripping from the branches of the big willows along the curving drive where I was parked. I walked behind her along the brick path to the drive, admiring the way her hips swiveled beneath the thin material, despite the limp. She'd been limping the night of the Elmore murder, when I'd spoken to her, but it seemed less pronounced now.

I went ahead and opened the passenger door. Lucas was sprawled gracelessly, his head lolling toward us, one hand between his legs. His sister's lips compressed to a thin line as she noticed the cut on his forehead. She glanced impassively at the woman in the backseat, then reached over and put a hand on her brother's shoulder, shaking him lightly.

"Rob," she said. "Rob, wake up."

His eyes came open, took a moment to focus, and then drifted shut again as a ragged smile formed on his lips. "Hi, sis," he murmured.

She gave me a helpless look.

"I'll carry him in," I said.

He was heavy, but under the gaze of Clarice Lucas I felt compelled to pretend he wasn't. It was hard making the last few steps at the top of the stairs look effortless, but I managed, and then tried not to drop him too roughly on the bed. We undressed him together, not speaking, both a little embarrassed, and then Clarice coaxed him into his blue silk pajamas while I pretended to study the wallpaper. She went to the adjoining bathroom for a damp washrag, then sat beside him on the bed for a moment, sponging his forehead and cheeks. It looked like something she'd done before.

"What do you want me to do with the woman?" I asked.

She gazed at me thoughtfully for a moment, then said, "Bring her in and put her on the sofa downstairs. I'll see to her."

I went back down and managed to drag the woman out of

the car, blanket and all, and lug her into the living room. She was dead to the world, and she had a death grip on the blanket. It was a lot of carrying for one night, and my back was getting stiff. I did some quick toe touches and some stretches while out of Clarice's sight, then went back up to Lucas's room. I stood silently in the doorway for a moment, watching Clarice dab at his face, her expression sad. The room was actually pretty Spartan for a guy like Lucas. There was a wooden armchair in one corner, a simple chest of drawers with a mirror on top, and a little cabinet with a lamp on it beside the head of the bed. Beside the lamp was a framed photo of a voluptuous blond woman in a low-cut evening dress, with a taunting half smile on her face.

"Who's that?" I asked.

Clarice jerked, startled. "What?" She looked where I was looking. "Oh. That's Betty June, Rob's wife." There was something carefully casual in her use of the name, perhaps masking distaste.

"Where's she? I didn't know he was married."

Clarice got up and took the washrag back to the bathroom, then began turning off lights, ushering me toward the hallway.

Once she'd closed the bedroom door behind her, she said, "Betty June is dead. She died about a year ago, right downstairs. During one of her parties." I knew from the way she said it that Betty June had given a lot of parties, that Clarice hadn't much liked them, and that Clarice was maybe even a little pleased that she'd checked out in the middle of one of them.

"What killed her?" I asked.

"Congenital heart defect. Previously undiscovered. Just keeled right over in the middle of a conversation. As it happened, her personal physician was at the party, so he was right on the spot. But he said she'd probably been dead before she hit the floor. He was very distraught, not having diagnosed the condition, although I'm not sure there's anything that could have been done about it.''

"Maybe cut down the partying," I said.

Clarice gave me a little smile and led me down the stairs to the foyer. We stood side by side for a moment, looking at the unconscious woman on the big white sofa in the living room.

"I get the impression you didn't like Betty June much," I said.

Clarice sighed. "I've never been very good at hiding my feelings," she said, then shrugged. "Really, she was all right in her way. She was what Rob wanted, anyway, and that's all that mattered. Flashy blonde, drop-dead figure, good dancer, great conversationalist. All the moves. Rob was crazy about her. I didn't think he'd ever get over her death. It knocked him for a loop. Getting him back to where he is now, campaigning again, thinking about the future . . . it's been a struggle.''

"I'm not sure he's quite over it yet," I said, glancing toward the living room.

"Yes," she said. "That's not really Rob's style. Or it didn't used to be."

"He really loved his wife," I said.

She nodded slowly, as though still amazed by the fact. "But he didn't get much back," she said. "I don't think Betty June really loved anybody but Betty June." She shook her head and her lower lip trembled, but she brought it under control. She looked back up the stairs. "Rob's really a fine man," she said. "He is. I never understood how he could feel what he did for Betty June, but he did. I just wish he could let her go now, forget her."

"He won't forget her," I said. "He might get past it eventually."

She gave me a long look and then smiled. "That sounds like the voice of experience," she said. "Or do cops get training in psychology?"

"Police work is training in psychology," I said.

"Yes, I suppose it is. Maybe that's what I should have done instead of going off to Barnard. It would have been cheaper."

"Your degree's in psychology?"

"Both of them, actually." Then she laughed, as though embarrassed to have said it.

"But you don't use it," I said.

"I don't use it to make money," she said. "Right now my job is taking care of Rob, getting him back on track, getting him elected."

"You're his campaign manager?"

She nodded. "I work cheap. And I believe in him. I really think the state will be better off with him in office. I know it probably doesn't look that way to you right now."

I shrugged. "I used to work vice in Kansas City," I said.

"The police course in abnormal psych," she said.

"I guess so. Except after a while the difference between the normal and the abnormal gets blurred. I've known people who've done a lot worse things than anything your brother's probably done, who were still decent people, in their way."

She looked at me a moment. "I can't decide if that's a comforting thought or not," she said.

"Well," I said, "on the other hand, there are people who never do much of anything you could say was bad, but who are still very bad people."

"Yes," she said. "I can believe that. Would you like a cup of coffee before you go?"

I hesitated, then nodded. I found I was enjoying talking to her. She turned and led me to the kitchen, and I noticed her limp again.

"How's the ankle?" I asked. "Getting better?"

She smiled ruefully, filling a little plastic pitcher with water and then putting it in the microwave. "Hope you don't mind crystals," she said.

14

"Got to be better than what they have in the machine at the station."

"Yes," she said. "The ankle's better. Mostly it just makes me feel stupid."

"How so?"

"Oh . . . it was after Rob found Bill Elmore's body and called the police. I was upstairs here, just getting out of the shower, and I heard the sirens and looked out and saw the crowd forming, so I went out on the landing, with a towel around me, and just then our neighbor, Millie Reynolds, leaned in the front door and shouted something. She was telling me Bill was dead, of course, but for some reason I thought she was yelling fire, that one of the houses in the block was on fire, you know? And here I was standing naked and all these houses are old and wooden and . . . well, anyway, I ran and got a robe and threw it half on and then tripped on it coming back out and slammed my leg against the banister post at the top. Actually, I'm lucky I didn't fall down the stairs and kill myself. Then you would have had two bodies to worry about."

"But yours would have been a lot more attractive," I said.

She gave me a slow smile and just then the bell on the microwave went off. She got up and poured steaming water into two thick mugs and added spoonfuls of coffee crystals. She put one of the mugs in front of me, with a spoon beside it. I stirred it.

"Cream and sugar?"

"Artificial sweetener, if you got it," I said. "Got to keep my boyish figure."

She grinned. "Yes," she said. "You ought to." She found a box of sweetener packets in a cupboard and handed me three of them, then sat down across from me. She slipped the red headband off, seeming to remember it suddenly, and set it on the table beside her coffee cup.

For some reason that made me feel vaguely uncomfortable. She was an attractive, intelligent woman and I enjoyed being there with her, but I already had a girlfriend, sort of, and we already had enough problems. It was Marcie's brother who'd been charged in the Elmore killing.

"That boy they arrested," Clarice said, as though she'd been reading my mind. "Does it really look like he did it?"

I shrugged. "I guess so," I said. "It's not my case." In fact, I'd started out working it, then had begged off when everything had started pointing to Eddie.

She shook her head and took a dainty, exploratory sip of coffee.

"It's so sad," she said. It looked like she really did feel badly about it.

"Elmore's death, you mean?" I asked.

"Oh, well, that too, of course. But I was really talking about the boy. I'd seen him a couple of times, you know, around Bill's place. He was always polite. Kind of sweet and shy, really. It's hard to imagine him killing someone."

I nodded. I agreed with her, but it was sometimes that way.

I put down the coffee cup and stood up. "I better be going," I said. "You need any help with the woman?"

Clarice shook her head. "I'll let her sleep it off, then give her some money—for her trouble, you know—and send her home in a cab."

"How much money you think you'll have to give her?" I asked. "For her trouble?"

She smiled over the top of her coffee cup. "Not too much, I don't think," she said. "Thank you for helping Rob."

I shrugged, remembering the unmarked pill bottle in my pocket. "He needs to be more careful," I said.

"Yes," she said forcefully. "He does. I'll see to that."

CHAPTER
THREE

The wind had died down while I'd sat in the Lucas kitchen. It was still cool, but muggy now. I felt cheated, and I knew that and the clamminess would only keep me awake if I went straight home, that I'd end up lying on my back in the dark, thinking about how I'd gotten here, whether I'd ever feel completely comfortable again, no matter where I was, and that, eventually, would start me thinking about Terry Gardens and Doolie Waters and what had happened in Kansas City.

So I went to the office instead, and hung my jacket over the back of the wooden swivel chair, and got out the Elmore file and looked through it, putting my feet up on the desk. It was Captain Mike Farrar, my immediate boss, who was in charge of the investigation, though there really hadn't been much to it. Elmore had been found on the floor of his den with his brains beaten in. The murder weapon had been a heavy glass candy dish. Elmore hadn't had any local relatives or close friends. The closest person to him, in fact, had been Eddie Skubitz, who did odd jobs for Elmore, and who had disappeared immediately after the murder. We'd put out a pickup order on him and the highway patrol had found him hitchhiking north, without any luggage, on Highway 50, up by Emporia. He'd had two hundred dollars in new twenties in his wallet, which he claimed Elmore had given him to buy a new suit. He denied killing Elmore, or knowing who killed him, though he admitted he'd seen the body, which was why he'd run. He'd done a short stretch at the Boys' Industrial Reformatory at Hutchinson, a year or so before, for a break-in, and he'd figured he'd get blamed for this, too. He was right. Ever since we'd brought him back and booked him, he'd clammed up, refusing to add anything to what he'd already said, even to tell us about seeing the body. Marcie was convinced he was innocent, but she also believed he'd been innocent of the break-in he'd been sent up for before. In that case, he'd been caught within a block of the scene, with three other, slightly older boys, who had had the goods on them. They'd first claimed to have found the stuff on the street, where someone else had dumped it, but then later a couple of them had admitted the burglary, and all four had gone up—the older boys to Lansing and Eddie to the reformatory. I hadn't been around then; I'd come to Elk Rapids while Eddie was still inside.

Footsteps sounded in the hallway outside and Mike Farrar came into the office. He had his jacket flung over his shoulder and his light blue shirt was splotched with moisture. His shoulder holster was old and frayed and he had a bandage wrapped around one hand. He was almost sixty, two months away from mandatory retirement, which I supposed he must be dreading, since he seemed to spend most of his time at the station. His wife had Alzheimer's and lived at a care home in a little town seven miles down the highway. Mike was nominally my boss, but he'd pretty much let me run things in the detective division since Chief Bullard had brought me down from Kansas City.

"I saw the light on," he said. He slumped down in the straight chair on the other side of the desk and gave me a tired smile.

"What happened to your hand?" I asked.

He looked at it as though he'd forgotten it was bandaged.

"We had a cutting at one of the bars out east," he said. "Couple of kids arguing over a game, if you can believe that. One of those electronic things."

"How'd you get involved?"

"I was just having a drink, on my way home. Had a couple of beers, decided I'd give the uniforms a hand, you know? No fool like an old fool."

"You get cut?"

He laughed. "One of 'em bit me when I was putting him in the squad car. I'm gettin' too old for this shit." It was something he said a lot lately.

"Old ladies help you across the street nowadays, do they?"

"That ain't the worst of it," he said. "The young ones don't run from me anymore." He leaned forward and peered at my desk through his bifocals. "That the Elmore file?"

"Yeah. I happened to run into Rob Lucas this evening. Just got to thinking about it."

Mike shrugged. "You can have it back, if you want it," he said sourly.

"You don't like it?" I asked.

He looked off toward one of the windows and fiddled absentmindedly with the bandage on his hand. "I don't like sending up a kid like Eddie for a thing like this," he said. " 'Specially this close to retirement. It'll leave me with a bad taste in my mouth."

"It's a problem for me, too," I said.

He waved a hand in dismissal. "Yeah, I know, I know. I'm just bitching, that's all."

We were both silent for a moment. It seemed like a moment when I could ask something that I'd wondered about for a while.

"Captain," I said, "how did you feel about Bullard bringing me in here the way he did? Did it bother you?"

He blinked at me behind the glasses, and scratched under his arm. "Why should it?" he asked.

"Well . . . you've been with the department your whole career. . . ."

He laughed. "You mean, bringing my successor in while I'm still here? That's a good word, ain't it? Successor? Makes me sound like a fucking king or something."

"Is that what he told you?" I asked. "That I was your successor?"

"Nah. Bullard don't talk that way. But it's pretty obvious, ain't it? Town like this, we don't figure to hire somebody with the experience you had, up in K.C. I mean, obviously you're not gonna be a lieutenant your whole life. Shit, I figure there's a pretty good chance you're gonna be Bullard's successor, too."

I thought about that. I couldn't figure out whether the prospect pleased me or not. I still wasn't used to the idea of being a cop in Elk Rapids instead of Kansas City. None of it still seemed quite real to me.

"You know why I left KC?" I asked. That was something else we'd never talked about before.

Mike inspected his fingernails. "You mean the pimp that got killed? Yeah, I heard something about that." He spoke offhandedly, the way suspects will when they finally admit to something embarrrassing.

"His name was Doolie Waters," I said. "I got involved with one of his girls. Her name was Terry Gardens."

Mike fidgeted with his holster as though it chafed him. "Those things happen, I guess," he said. "Big city like that . . ."

"She was only spending time with me to protect Doolie." I said. "But I was too dumb to get it. She finally had to tell me. I guess I was getting on her nerves. And she made it very clear. No chance of misunderstanding. So I went out and got drunk and then I went and visited Doolie, hoping he'd give me an excuse. And he did; he said something, I don't remember what. And so I beat him to death. I don't think I meant to kill him. That's something else I can't quite remember. Anyway, it doesn't matter much what I meant to do, does it?''

Mike didn't say anything for a moment. He gave me a puzzled, slightly pained look, wondering why I was saying these things to him, what he was supposed to say about it. I didn't know. It was the first time I'd told it to anybody that way, straight out, not cutting corners, and I was already wishing I hadn't. "I don't suppose anyone'll miss him much," Mike said tentatively.

"Terry will," I said. It was astonishing how much it still hurt to admit that. "Anyway," I added, "he didn't deserve to die. And it wasn't my place to kill him. Those are facts. They don't go away."

"Shit happens," Mike said. "You put it behind you and go on. That's all you can do." He looked away from me as he said it. We both knew how lame it sounded.

"Doesn't somebody have to pay?" I asked him.

He sighed. "That's the theory," he said. "Doesn't always work out that way, I guess." For a second, he seemed to be thinking of something else, then he gave me a quick glance, to see if I'd noticed, and said, "Hell, you're still pretty young. You still got time going for you, if you don't piss it all away. My problem was, I stuck around one place too long, 'til I got to be older than everyone else. I'm two years older than Underchief Perkins, so there was no way I could outlast him, and I'll probably be dead before Bullard retires. But you're in pretty good position. Another two years, you can move into the underchief's job, if you want it. Not that it amounts to squat, except for the extra pay."

I didn't say anything. He was obviously changing the subject, and I decided to let him.

"You know," Mike said, "All I ever really wanted was to get out of this shitty town."

"So why'd you stay?" I asked.

He shrugged. "There's only so many ways out of a place like this. I wasn't very smart in school. I wasn't a good enough football player. I didn't have a rich uncle. Being a cop seemed like it might be a possibility. Work here awhile, then move on to Pittsburg or Joplin, then maybe someplace bigger, Wichita or Oklahoma City or even K.C. or St. Louis. But it never happened. I did apply for some things, but there was always someone a little sharper, and then after a while there was always someone a little younger.'' He shrugged. ''And besides, Eleanor and me, our families are all around here. I don't know. Maybe Elk Rapids was just my speed, all along.'' His voice didn't sound bitter; he had a pleasant smile on his face as he spoke, as though there was something about it all that pleased him, some private joke. ''Anyway,'' he said, ''now I'm finally getting out. Two more months and I'm gone.''

''Gone? You mean leaving town? Not just the department?''

''Fuckin' A. Eleanor and me, we been talkin' about movin' to the Southwest. Arizona. New Mexico. It's nice down there. Warm. Beautiful scenery. We went on a couple of tours down there, years ago, liked it a lot. No snow. Not a lot of people around. I could handle that.''

He always talked about his wife as though she were still the same as she'd always been, still living at home with him. Maybe he really did go out to the nursing home and talk to her about his retirement plans. I wondered whether he planned to put her in a home after they moved, or take care of her himself. From what I'd heard, the home she was in wasn't the greatest place—the state health department had been on them more than once for neglect—but it was the nearest one to Elk Rapids, and probably all Mike could afford on a cop's salary. Moving to a warmer climate was probably just a pipe dream.

''Sounds great,'' I said. ''I guess I just assumed you'd stay in Elk Rapids, be close to the grandkids.''

''Well . . .'' He bent his head back slightly and scratched his neck. ''We've talked about that, too, of course. But . . .

22

what the hell. You only go around once, like they say. Might as well go for the gusto.''

I nodded. "You deserve it," I said.

"Yeah," he said happily. "I think I do." He stood up. "I better get my butt on home," he said. "You too. Looks like you could use some sleep."

After he was gone, I sat for a while longer, looking at the photos in the Elmore folder. There were three of Elmore sprawled across the shag rug in his den, the back of his head a bloody mass. He was wearing suit pants, a white shirt and tie, but his feet were bare. Another photo showed the thick glass candy dish with smears of blood along one edge. According to the autopsy report, he'd been hit several times, over and over. It looked as though the first blow had only stunned him, and he'd knocked over the coffee table, maybe trying to defend himself, or get at his attacker, and then the next blow had put him out, but the killer had kept on hitting him, in a frenzy or maybe a panic, until he was dead. I tried to imagine Eddie doing that. I could. But then, sometimes it seemed to me I could imagine anyone doing anything.

I thought about Elmore himself. If there was any mystery in this case, he was it. He'd come to Elk Rapids just a few months before I had, and had bought into Skahan Motors, the Ford dealership, although Mack Skahan still ran it. It had just been a source of income for Elmore. What we'd found out during the investigation was that no one really knew him, or even where he came from, and his personal effects were no help, either. There were no letters from other places, no little black book with distant phone numbers in it. He had a modest bank account, and no real property outside of the big house he'd bought on Circle Street. Everything in the house had been new, but not particularly expensive. He appeared to have no hobbies. He went to parties when invited, gave an occasional party of his own—always big ones, paying back everyone who'd invited him—and played golf at the country

23

club, but with no regular group, just whoever was looking for a game.

The only thing that didn't fit was Eddie. Eddie had done his eight months at the reformatory, had gotten out a year ago, had hung out with Marcie for a month or so, looking for a job, finding nothing, and then—according to what Eddie had told Marcie—had run into Elmore at the county courthouse one day when he was checking in with his parole officer. He hadn't known what Elmore was doing there, and Elmore couldn't tell us now. Eddie said he'd come out of the parole office and Elmore had been waiting for the elevator. Waiting together, they'd struck up a conversation, and it had continued in the elevator and into the parking lot outside, and Elmore had offered him a ride, which he'd accepted, and by the time they'd gotten to where he was going, Eddie had a job. By all accounts, including Eddie's, the job, apart from occasional errands and odd jobs, had really amounted to hanging around with Elmore and listening to a lot of advice on how to act and dress and talk. After his death, everyone agreed that Bill Elmore had been a wonderful man to try to help Eddie the way he had, and how horrible it was that Eddie had turned on him that way, killed him for a measly two hundred dollars. Clarice Lucas, it occurred to me, was the only one of Elmore's acquaintances who seemed to have any trouble believing Eddie had done it. Maybe she was the only one of them who had paid any attention to Eddie before that. I wondered what she'd thought of Elmore. Perhaps I'd ask her sometime.

I closed the folder and put it back in the file cabinet in the dayroom, and then went downstairs and through the tunnel to the sheriff's office across the alley.

The county jail occupies the two floors above the sheriff's office. The second floor is used mostly as a drunk tank and a holding pen for those awaiting trail or waiting to be bailed out. As a murder suspect—something fairly rare in Elk Rapids—they'd put Eddie on the third floor, in a block of cells that was otherwise empty.

I checked my gun with the guard and he buzzed me through the metal door, then used the remote switch to open Eddie's cell door. Eddie's cell was the next to the last one at the other end of the narrow hall. He'd been asleep on the lower bunk, but the opening door had awakened him, and he was sitting up and putting on his glasses when I got there.

He was a short boy with a thin face, and the thick wire-rims gave him a slightly scholarly, slightly goofy look. His sister had blond hair, but his was light brown with a reddish cast. It was warm in the jail and he had taken his shirt off, revealing his skinny, white, hairless chest. He wore only the gray jail trousers—about two sizes too big for him—with the drawstring tied in a droopy bow at his waist. He smiled shyly when he saw who it was. "Hey, Johnny," he said.

"Want to take a walk?" I asked him.

He nodded eagerly and got up and came out in the hall, a little hesitantly, as though he wasn't sure it was allowed, but figured it might be, since I was there. We turned away from the blank wall at the end of the hall and walked back toward the guard station. The little window was empty, the guard not bothering to watch us. Nobody expected Eddie to cause any trouble.

Marcie had told me his previous conviction had been a result of his hanging around with some older boys, trying to fit in, and I could believe it. He reminded me of a kid I'd known in high school, hanging around the edges of a group of guys, laughing along with everyone else even when it seemed obvious he didn't understand what the joke was, even when he suspected it was on him. I remembered telling a dirty joke in the locker room once, after gym class, and everyone laughing and then going to their lockers and this kid—I couldn't remember his name—sitting down beside me and asking, "And what did he do then, Johnny?" I couldn't

25

remember the joke, but I knew I had said, "He screwed her. What do you think?"

And the kid had smiled and nodded, and said, "Yeah, sure, I know that. But I mean, exactly what did he do?"

I'd realized then that he hadn't known, but I'd been too self-conscious to try to explain it to him with the other guys around—and I could see some of them were listening, giving each other grins—and so I'd pretended it was some kind of joke he was making, given him some smart-ass remark, waved him away, and he'd had sense enough to go along with that and laugh and drift off to his own locker, and I'd wondered how a kid could get to be high school age without knowing something like that.

I was pretty sure that wasn't the case with Eddie, or with anybody anymore. Nowadays the kids not only knew everything by the time they were in high school, they'd probably done most of it. But I doubted that Eddie had done very much. According to Marcie, he'd never had any girlfriends. For that matter, the only friend of any kind he'd had—apart from the tough guys he'd tried to attach himself to—had been another kid whose parents were dead, who'd lived with an aunt and uncle in one of the better parts of town. "They seemed to be each other's only friends," Marcie had said. The other kid had been smart, though, and had gone off to college after graduation and never come back to Elk Rapids. I wondered about that friendship. Had it just been the fact that they were both orphans, or was there something in Eddie that only this kid and Marcie—and maybe Bill Elmore—had seen?

"This is like in the hospital," Eddie said. "When they let you get up and walk down the hall."

"When were you in the hospital?" I asked.

"I had my appendix out in junior high. And my tonsils before that. I remember I couldn't eat anything but ice cream for a while."

I nodded. I wondered if he ever got ice cream here, but I

didn't want to ask. We walked in silence for a while, turning back toward his cell.

"You going to ask me stuff?" he asked.

I shook my head. "That's not why I came up," I said. "I just came to see how you're doing."

He nodded. "That's great," he said.

"Of course," I said, "I do think you ought to start answering Captain Farrar's questions. I think you'd be better off."

He frowned and stopped walking. I stopped, too, and looked at him. "I been thinking about that," he said.

"Good," I said. "What have you thought?"

He made a wry face. "My lawyer," he said, "he thinks I should . . . bargain?"

"Plea bargain," I said.

"Right. Plea bargain." He shook his head. "But then I'd have to say I did it," he said.

I nodded. I didn't say anything. I knew I should probably try to push him in that direction, too, but I found that I didn't want to. He was an easy kid to push, and he seemed to be making a real effort to work it out on his own.

"And I didn't do it," he added. His voice was soft, not as though he were trying to persuade me, but just as though it were the bottom line of an argument he'd been having with himself. At that instant, I believed him. And that made me wonder something I hadn't wondered before: If he really didn't do it, why wouldn't he tell us what he knew?

"Have you told your lawyer anything you haven't told us?" I asked. "I'm not asking you to tell me what it is," I added quickly. "Just whether you've talked to him more."

He shook his head, apparently not bothered by the question. We came around to his cell once more and he stepped back inside and sat down on the bunk, putting his chin in his hands. There was nothing else to sit on in the cell, so I leaned against the bars with my hands in my pockets.

"So," I said, "he's telling you you have two choices. You

can plead to a lesser charge—manslaughter, something like that—or you can stick with an innocent plea and take a chance on being convicted of murder one. A pretty good chance, I'd say.''

He nodded. ''That's what I been thinking about,'' he said. ''But it's not that simple.''

''Why not?''

''If I plead guilty, I have to tell them all about it.''

''That's true,'' I said. ''What's the problem?''

He shook his head.

I thought about it. There were two reasons I could think of for not wanting to talk in Eddie's situation. One was that spilling the beans would put you in a worse spot, but I didn't see how that could be in Eddie's case. Even if he'd really killed Elmore in cold blood, he was smart enough to come up with a way of describing it that would fit a manslaughter charge. Dumber guys than him did that all the time. The other possible reason was that telling all you knew would make it obvious you *didn't* do it—that someone else did.

''Eddie,'' I said, ''are you protecting somebody?''

He gave me a quick, surprised look, but then looked away and shook his head. I couldn't tell if the surprised look meant that I'd guessed right or that he was really surprised by the question.

''If you are,'' I said, ''are they worth doing time for?''

He licked his lips. ''There ain't nobody,'' he said.

There were two reasons I knew of that a guy like Eddie would protect somebody—loyalty and fear. Was Eddie being a stand-up guy for one of his old buddies, maybe somebody he'd invited over to Elmore's place to impress—which was just the kind of thing Eddie might do—or was he afraid of someone, someone he thought was powerful enough to pay him back if he talked? Whatever the case, he looked to me like someone who was getting ready to crack. Which meant I ought to get Mike Farrar involved, get it on the record when he did, instead of just futzing around on my own.

"Eddie," I said, "I gotta go." I took my hands out of my pockets and stepped through the open cell door.

He stood up and followed me, not coming out.

"Anything you want me to say to Marcie?" I asked. "Anything you want her to bring you?"

He shook his head distractedly. "I'm okay," he said. "Thanks for coming to visit."

I nodded, resisted an impulse to put a hand on his bare shoulder, and turned away. I was nearly to the guardroom door when he called my name.

"Johnny?"

I turned around.

"I want to . . . I'd like to ask you something. Private, you know?"

I walked back. "You want me to promise I won't tell anybody?" I asked. "I don't know if I can do that."

"No, it's just . . . okay. This is what it is. This is like . . . imaginary, you know?"

"Hypothetical," I said.

"Hypothetical. Right." He frowned and went on. "Say you got this man and wife," he said. "The guy is . . . everyone thinks he's a great guy, you know? But at home, just him and his wife, he's . . . real mean. To his wife, I mean. Nobody else. He orders her around, talks mean to her, makes her do stuff she doesn't like to do." He'd been staring at me intensely as he talked, but on that last phrase his eyes slid away from mine. "You get what I'm talking about?" he asked.

"I think so."

"So one time, something happens. He . . . does something worse than usual. I don't know. Something. And so she hits him. Just . . . without thinking . . . just . . ."

"A reflex," I suggested.

"A reflex," he repeated. "And the guy dies." He squinted at me behind the thick glasses. "Could that be self-defense?" he asked.

29

"Sure," I said. "But you mean, she just hits him once and he dies. You don't mean she hits him over and over again till she's sure he's dead."

Eddie frowned, chewing at his lower lip. "Once she got going . . ." he said.

"I know," I said. "She couldn't stop. She panicked." Or she saw an opportunity and took it, I thought. I knew too well how that could work. "Whatever," I said. "It wouldn't be murder one, not premeditated. But it wouldn't exactly be self-defense, either."

"What would it be?" he asked.

"Some kind of manslaughter, I guess. But . . ."

"She'd still go to prison," Eddie said.

"Probably not very long," I said. "Maybe not at all. It would depend on the judge, the circumstances. She'd probably get probation, mostly. Maybe get sent to a hospital instead of prison."

Eddie nodded.

"There's something else to consider," I said. "If it was during the commission of a crime, it might still be murder."

He blinked at me uncomprehendingly.

"If she stole something from him," I said. "Something like that, after she killed him."

"Why would she . . ." he began, and then he gave a little smile and nodded. "Oh," he said, "you mean the two hundred dollars." He shook his head. "I wasn't talking about me," he said, "about all that. It was just something I'd been thinking about. To pass the time, you know?"

I nodded and waited for him to say something else, but he didn't. After a moment, he turned and went back to his bunk and sat down.

"Eddie," I said, "there's no percentage in doing time for somebody else. Whether you care about them that much, or whether you're scared of them. Either way."

He nodded. "I am scared of going back," he said. "I know it won't be Hutch this time. It'll be Lansing." He swallowed. "But I got through it before," he said. "I know how to handle it."

"Anytime you want to talk," I told him, "send me a message through the guard. I'll come up as soon as I can."

"Thanks, Johnny," he said. "Tell Marcie I love her."

"You can tell her yourself," I said. "I'm sure she'll be here tomorrow, like she is every day."

"Yeah," he said. "I guess she will." He gave me one of those goofy smiles.

Before I went back to my car, I crossed back over to the police station and left a note on Mike's desk, telling him I thought Eddie might be protecting someone else, and that he looked like he might also be getting ready to talk.

I thought about calling Marcie. She might know something that would help. But she'd be asleep by now, and it could wait until morning. I'd have breakfast out at the truck stop, where she worked as a waitress, and tell her then. I liked thinking about that. It would be the best news she'd had since Eddie had been arrested. Walking back to my car, I thought maybe I'd be able to get some sleep after all.

CHAPTER
FOUR

I did sleep well, but when I got to the truck stop, Marcie wasn't there. She'd called in sick. Vonda, the hostess, put me in my regular corner booth, the one I'd taken over when I'd come down from K.C. two years before, so I could survey the strangers around me, try to figure out what kind of place I'd come to after a lifetime in the city, and watch the big trucks rolling off the interstate ramp into the huge gravel parking lot outside.

Now there weren't as many strangers as there'd been then, though I still felt something of an outsider. Maybe I'd always feel that way. Dexter Gennaro, the owner, was in his own corner booth, just beyond the cash register, with a bunch of cronies who gathered for breakfast every morning to shoot the bull about politics and crop prices and who was cheating on who down at the VFW hall. Dexter saw me and gave me a wave, and I waved back. I'd met people around Elk Rapids who didn't like him, but from what I could tell, it was just the usual jealousy of someone who started out the same place they had and had made a pile, while they hadn't. Mostly what I'd heard was that he was a skinflint, that he paid his help next to nothing. Marcie confirmed that, but she said the tips from the truckers still made it the best waitressing job in town. To me, Dexter just seemed like a nice old guy who enjoyed hobnobbing with the big shots—the other big shots—in Elk Rapids. He looked a little like Gerald Ford. You could tell he'd been some kind of athlete once—one of the other cops had told me he'd heard he'd been a boxer when he was young—but he had one of those soft, open faces, the kind that make it hard to tell whether someone is smart or dumb. When he saw you, he'd give a little smile, or a look of concern, depending on how you looked, like an old uncle who just wants what's best for you.

Reneta waited on me. She was Hispanic, short, and round. Her family had lived in Elk Rapids as long as any, but people still asked her where she came from. She was the best waitress at the truck stop and usually worked the special back room of the coffee shop, where only working drivers could sit, where the coffee was free and there was a telephone near every booth, and a jukebox playing country songs that could only be heard distantly out here in the main part. Right now I could almost hear Steve Earle singing about Guitar Town, the bass thumping in the walls at the end of each verse.

"How come you're out here?" I asked Reneta. "Been demoted?"

"It's 'cause your girlfriend didn't come in this morning," she said. She smiled, but I could tell she was really pissed—probably a little pissed at me, by association.

After she'd taken my order, she went over to the big center table where half a dozen highway patrol troopers and sheriff's deputies were hanging their walkie-talkies over the backs of the chairs, settling in for breakfast with a lot of creaking of leather and wood, giving me little nods as they noticed me there, then kidding with Reneta. She kidded right back, but her eyes never lost their cold, concentrated look. This was serious business for her. She was the kind of waitress who could work six full tables at once and get everything right and keep all the coffee cups filled.

Marcie wasn't that good, and she didn't take naturally to the kidding of the truckers and the cops. That had probably been one of the reasons we'd gotten to be friends. I'd just been a single man, coming in every morning, keeping to myself, not making many demands. After a couple of weeks she'd started bringing me the coffee and the glass of tomato juice and the toast before I'd even ordered. After a couple more weeks, she'd started hanging around my table when she wasn't busy, making small talk. Finally I'd asked her out and things had gone pretty quickly after that. It wasn't until the first night I'd stayed over at her place that she'd found out I was a cop. That was the same night I'd found out she had a brother in the reformatory. It had been a surprising night for both of us, but it hadn't kept us from seeing each other again.

Someone was standing beside my table. I looked up and saw one of the sheriff's deputies, Rudy Bannerman. Reneta was hovering just behind him with my order. She gave him a nudge and he glanced at her and then stepped aside, looking embarrassed, and she started laying the plates out, quickly and efficiently, in front of me.

"Sorry to bother you, lieutenant," Bannerman said, "but we just got a call asking if we'd seen you. Your dispatcher's trying to run you down."

"Thanks," I said. I took time to put the sweetener in the coffee and stir it and take a sip, and then I got up and went into the truckers' section and grabbed the nearest wall phone. There was a skinny guy with a big cowboy hat and a leather vest sitting in the booth, and he gave me a frown, but then shrugged and went back to his chili omelette. I dialed the station.

"Captain Farrar wants you to 10–43 with him at the jail," the dispatcher told me.

"What's up?"

"He didn't say, lieutenant. Sounded urgent, though."

I went back to the table and picked up the check, flipping a couple of dollars into the glass ashtray. On the way to the counter, Reneta passed me, carrying somebody's order in one hand and a coffee pot in the other.

"You're not gonna eat it?" she asked.

"Don't worry," I said. "I left your tip."

She gave me her cold smile.

I began to suspect what had happened when I saw the yellow emergency vehicle sitting in front of the sheriff's office, its rear doors open.

"Shit," I said under my breath, and got out and went up the steps to the lobby.

The door to the guardroom on the third floor was standing open and there were cops and fire department medics crowded into the narrow hallway. I wormed my way through.

Mike Farrar knelt beside one of the medics on the floor of Eddie's cell. The medic had been giving Eddie mouth-to-mouth, and as I got there, he rocked back on his heels and shook his head. Eddie lay on his back, his features puffy and distorted, almost unrecognizable. His glasses lay on the concrete floor in the corner, resting on the lenses but apparently unbroken. He was still wearing only the gray trousers, but now the matching shirt was tied by one sleeve to the welded railing of the upper bunk, and the other sleeve had been twisted and knotted to form a kind of makeshift rope. Sitting on the lower bunk was a food tray with pancakes and bacon, untouched, and a small plastic glass of orange juice that had fallen on its side and spilled. There was a strong smell of excrement in the cell, one of the several odors of sudden death.

Mike looked up at me, his eyes watery and unfocused. He looked about a hundred years old. He didn't say anything. The medic closed his kit and stood up. I saw the purple marks left by the noose along the underside of Eddie's jaw.

Mike started to get to his feet, then seemed to have some trouble. I stepped forward and put a hand under his arm, and he leaned into me a little, getting up. There was a smaller, cleaner bandage on the hand where he'd been bitten the night before.

"Let's get out of here," he said.

The guard was standing out in the hall, looking embarrassed and superfluous.

"Were you on duty?" I asked him.

He nodded.

"When did you check him last?" I heard myself snapping at him, taking the anger out on him.

He started to say something, then had to clear his throat. I realized then that he wasn't much older than Eddie, and that he was scared. Probably the first time he'd seen something like this.

"Captain Farrar . . ." he began.

"I was up here talking to the kid this morning," Mike said. "Because of your note. Then they brought his breakfast in, so I went over across the street to get some of my own. He must have done it right after I left."

"I come around to collect the tray," the guard said. "Usually, he'd slide it out in the hall when he was done, but it got to be almost an hour, and he hadn't yet, so I went to get it." He made a helpless gesture with his hands.

"It's not your fault, son," Mike said. "If he was going to do it, he'd have done it sooner or later. And nobody expected him to."

The guard gave me a wide-eyed look and I nodded, and Mike and I went on out through the guard station and down the stairs.

"I don't get it," I said, when we were back in the dayroom. "What'd he say when you talked to him this morning? Did something happen?"

Mike shook his head. "Nothing," he said. "It was just like always. He was polite, and ready to talk about anything except the murder. What gave you the idea he was ready to start talking?"

36

I told him what we'd talked about the night before, Eddie's hypothetical question and his doubts about copping a plea.

"He seemed more concerned about having to tell everything he knew than he did about pleading guilty," I said.

Mike nodded thoughtfully. "It's hard to see who he'd be protecting," he said, "unless it was one of those punks he used to hang out with. And I can't see Eddie taking a murder rap for one of those guys."

"Could have been somebody he was afraid of," I said.

Mike shrugged. "It's academic now," he said.

"What do you mean?"

"I don't see any reason he'd kill himself unless he did it. Do you?"

I thought about it. Suicide was the last thing I'd have expected from Eddie Skubitz, especially after our talk the night before. Maybe the talk about being able to handle prison had just been bravado, for my benefit.

"Sounds to me like he was trying out different possibilities, different ways out," Mike said. "And he couldn't come up with any he thought would work. By the time I talked to him, he'd clammed up again. He must've already decided to do it."

"Why wait?" I said. "Why not do it during the night? That's when they usually do it."

Mike shook his head sadly. "I don't know," he said. "Maybe he didn't want to do it in the dark. I wouldn't want to do it in the dark." For a second, he sounded like he knew what he was talking about, like someone who'd thought about it. For some reason, that made me angry again.

"I don't buy it," I said. "The kid I talked to last night was not someone getting ready to off himself."

Mike gave me a surprised look. "Weren't you ever wrong about something like that?" he asked softly.

I felt my face grow suddenly hot, as though I'd been slapped. For a second I thought he was talking about Terry

Gardens, but then I realized he wasn't. I took a deep breath and swallowed the anger.

"Yes," I said. "I have been."

"Someone's going to have to tell the sister," Mike said.

"Christ Jesus," I said. I sat down heavily in the wooden chair beside his desk.

"I'll do it if you want me to," he said. "Might be easier."

I shook my head.

"No," I said. "I've got to do it." I didn't know why that was true, exactly, but I knew it was. Maybe it was only that I was afraid Marcie would think less of me if I didn't. I shook my head, trying to make myself think like a cop. It was something I found myself having to do more and more in Elk Rapids. "You don't think there's enough reason to reopen the Elmore investigation?" I asked.

Mike shook his head wearily. It occurred to me that reopening a major murder investigation two months before he was due to retire was probably the last thing on earth he'd want to do. But I felt immediately ashamed for thinking that; Mike might be old and tired, but he was a pro.

"I think there's less reason now than there was before," Mike said. "I admit I wasn't convinced the kid did it, at least not on purpose, not premeditated. I kept hoping he'd spill something that would take him off the hook." He gave a heavy sigh. "But he didn't, and now he can't. And I can't help thinking that if there was anything he would have come up with it instead of killing himself. The fact is, the simplest explanation usually turns out to be the right one in this business, no matter how shitty it is."

I nodded. That was true. I'd liked Eddie. I'd wanted him to be innocent. That was why I'd begged off the investigation. And he'd known that, which was probably why he'd talked to me the way he had, instead of Mike, maybe trying out possibilities, as Mike said, and not finding any that worked for him. And I'd sensed he was hiding something, but because I'd liked him I'd taken it to mean he was protecting someone else, but maybe that was just me, wanting to find a better explanation. The fact was I had no new lead, no alternate suspect to offer. I got up, feeling old and creaky myself.

"I'll go see Marcie," I said. "She called in sick, so she ought to be at home."

He gave me an absentminded wave, but didn't look up as I went out.

In the hallway outside, an old geezer with whiskers and a jail trusty's outfit was on his hands and knees scrubbing the floor. Actually, he was holding the bottle of disinfectant in front of his face, studying the label.

"Don't do it, gramps," I said. "You'll throw up everything down to your kneecaps."

He gave me a guilty grin and went back to work.

As I went past Bullard's office, I heard him call my name. I stepped back and went in.

He was a neat, compact man. Back in Kansas City, four or five years before, he'd been the best detective in the department, clearly on his way to being chief of detectives. That was before a couple of junkies got the drop on him in an alley and worked him over, leaving him with a right arm that was paralyzed and useless. They'd taken something else from him, too—something less easy to identify. After he'd gotten out of the hospital, he'd tried a desk job for a while, but it hadn't worked out. For one thing, he hadn't been able to get along with anyone. The bluntness that worked for him as a detective didn't go over as well with the brass and their clerks. I didn't know all the details, but there'd been some sort of negotiations and he'd finally agreed to take early retirement with a disability pension. I hadn't realized he'd taken the Elk Rapids job until a couple of years later, when I'd found myself also taking a kind of forced retirement, and he'd called me up out of the blue and offered me my present job.

"I heard about the kid," he said. "I'm sorry. I know

you're close to his sister.'' He didn't sound particularly sorry—or particularly anything. He was just saying what one was supposed to say in this situation. Still, he'd called me in to say it.

"It was a surprise," I said. "I'd talked to him last night, and I had the impression he was ready to talk, that he might be protecting someone else."

Bullard gazed expressionlessly at me for a moment, then pulled a thin cigar out of his inside jacket pocket, moistened it, and lit it with a silver lighter that sat on his desk, doing it all easily with his left hand. His right hung straight down at his side.

"Why were you talking to him?" Bullard asked. "I thought you wanted off the case."

I shook my head. "It was just a visit," I said. "I liked the kid."

"Starting to like them can be a mistake," Bullard said. "You ought to know that better than anybody." He blew a smoke ring in the air in front of him, an old unconscious habit.

"This was different," I said, trying to keep my voice level and not quite succeeding.

His lips moved almost imperceptibly, perhaps a ghost of a smile, and he said, "They always are, aren't they? What made you think the kid was protecting someone?"

I recounted what I'd told Mike. He considered it and then shrugged.

"Interesting," he said, "but it doesn't point anywhere. And he had the money on him. Mike's probably right."

"I know," I said. "I just don't like it. It feels unfinished."

"It always does when something like this happens. But it isn't your problem. It's Mike's."

I nodded. I started to say something about how tired Mike seemed, about him being a short-timer, but I couldn't find any way to say it that wouldn't sound like a criticism, so I kept my mouth shut.

"Something else?" Bullard asked. His left hand was leafing through the papers on his desk.

"No," I said. I turned and went out.

CHAPTER
FIVE

In the same way that the neighborhood where the Lucases and William Elmore lived was called Circle Street, after the curving street that looped through it, the area where the Skubitz kids lived, on the south edge of town, was usually called Randall Drive. Randall Drive itself was a two-lane blacktop, slightly elevated, that ran from the interstate exit where Dexter Gennaro's truck stop was located to the old U.S. highway where it slanted past the southwest corner of town. There weren't actually many houses on Randall Drive itself, just dirt roads leading off into a small community of house trailers, shanties, and unpainted farmhouses—what would have been the other side of the tracks in another era.

The Skubitz home was actually in the better part of the Randall Drive neighborhood, a couple of blocks of shotgun bungalows, built shortly after the war for some of the more successful or more pretentious mine workers, back when Elk Rapids had been a company town, before all the coal had been stripped out and the companies had moved on.

Marcie and Eddie's parents had died when she was in high school and he was in junior high, and she had somehow hung on to the house and then had managed to keep it looking neat and clean among all the sagging porches and peeling paint that surrounded it.

I parked in the gravel drive that ran alongside the house, noticing that the lawn had gotten a little shaggier than usual. Since Eddie had gotten out of the reformatory, Marcie had gotten used to letting him do the mowing again, and his arrest had broken the routine. Now she'd have to let it grow or go back to mowing it herself.

Nobody answered when I knocked. The front door was standing open, but when I put my face against the screen to peer inside I saw no one in the big living room–dining room that stretched the length of the house, taking up most of its floor space. I opened the screen and went in. An ironing board was set up in front of the open windows along the side of the room, and there was a pile of laundry on the floor beside it, and a little fan blowing toward the place where the ironer would stand, but Marcie was nowhere in sight. I called her name and got no answer.

I went on through the house, but there was no one in any of the rooms. When I got to the kitchen and looked through the little window above the sink, I saw her standing outside in the backyard, beneath the big oak tree in the center. She wore an old sleeveless yellow dress, and the breeze that was blowing flared the skirt out to one side. She was barefoot and had her blond hair tied up in a tight bun. She was hugging herself, her hands clutching her bare arms at the shoulder, and her head was bent. It appeared that she might already know what had happened. The tree she was standing under had been an important part of her and her brother's childhood. They had swung from it, built a treehouse in its branches, and hidden things in the hollow on the far side.

I hesitated a moment, then took a breath and went out the back door and down the short wooden steps. She turned at the sound, saw who it was, and smiled. I knew from the smile that she hadn't heard the news yet, and the relief I hadn't even realized I'd been feeling vanished. I'd still have to do it.

"Hi, Johnny," she said. "How'd you know I was here?"

"They told me at the truck stop you called in sick."

She gave a sheepish grin, raising her eyebrows slightly. A strand of blond hair that had come loose from the bun fell down in front of one eye and she stuck her lower lip out and blew it aside. "Sometimes you just have to blow it off," she said.

I nodded. Actually, Marcie was normally a pretty conscientious worker, not the kind to take a fake sick day. But she'd done it once before, near the beginning of our relationship, when she'd been scheduled to work on a Saturday and had decided to spend the day with me instead. She'd felt so guilty about it, so afraid of being spotted by someone who knew she ought to be working, that we'd spent the whole day inside the house, which had been fine with me.

"It's hot," I said, stalling, looking around at the rest of the big backyard. There was a handmade brick patio at one corner of the house, with grass growing between the bricks here and there, and an old round metal table with a hole in the middle for an umbrella shaft. The umbrella and the folding chairs that went with the table would be in the rusting metal shed at the rear corner of the yard, along with the lawn mower. A clothesline stretched across the back of the yard, a pair of sheets billowing sluggishly in the breeze.

"There's ice water in the refrigerator," Marcie said. "Want a drink?"

"Sure," I said. I followed her back up the steps and into the kitchen. She opened the refrigerator and pulled out an old orange-juice bottle filled with water. I glimpsed a couple of cans of diet pop, packets of lunch meat and cheese, bowls covered by plastic wrap, a lone head of lettuce. I took the bottle from her, twisted the cap off, and took a drink. It had a funny taste, but not bad. I handed it back to her and she took a drink, holding it with both hands like a child, and then set it down on the counter. There were tiny beads of sweat on her forehead and cheeks.

I pulled a terry cloth dish towel from the rack beside the

stove and used it to wipe the sweat from her face and neck. She closed her eyes in automatic pleasure, and I leaned down and kissed the tip of her nose. She kissed me quickly on the lips before I could get away, putting her arms around my waist.

We stood like that for a moment and then I loosened her arms and said, "Let's go sit down. We need to talk."

She gave me a questioning look, but went ahead of me into the big room, where she perched on one end of the sagging sofa, tucking her legs up under her. I sat on the wooden rocker facing her.

"It's something about Eddie, isn't it?" she said. She looked apprehensive.

I nodded, unsure how to start.

"He confessed, didn't he?" she said, her voice suddenly full of anger and sorrow. I started to deny it, but she said, "I was afraid he was going to do something like that. He's so scared. And that lawyer they gave him . . ." She made a grimace of disgust.

"That's not it," I said, feeling miserable.

She looked at me in surprise. "What then?" she asked.

"Marcie," I said. "Shit." She stared at me while I tried to get the words together. "He's dead," I said at last. "He hanged himself in his cell."

She kept on staring at me for a moment with that surprised look, as though I'd just spoken in Swahili.

"He . . ." she said, and then the surprise went away and her face began to collapse in on itself. She got up from the sofa and I half rose, thinking she was coming to me for consolation, but instead she walked to the bedroom off the far end of the living room, went in, and closed the door behind her.

I sat back down, feeling foolish and guilty and not quite knowing why. Maybe just because I was a cop—one of them, from Marcie's point of view. Maybe it was also because I knew there was part of myself I'd always held back from

Marcie, the part that had never gotten over Terry Gardens, maybe never would, the part that was determined never to be fooled that badly again. Maybe if I'd been able to let go of that part, she'd have turned to me at this moment, instead of going into her bedroom to cry by herself.

I waited, feeling awkward and superfluous. After a while she came out again, her eyes red but her face composed, and went into the bathroom, closing that door behind her.

I got up and went back to the kitchen, where I had another drink of water and stared out the window at the big empty backyard. Beyond the clothesline at the far end there was a low ragged hedge, and beyond that a dirt road and then a scraggly field where some kind of grain was planted, the stalks short and bronze-tipped. I knew it wasn't corn, and it didn't look like what I thought wheat ought to look like. Maybe it was alfalfa. Or milo. After two years in Elk Rapids, I still didn't know what that was, or what it was used for, but I knew it was something they grew around here. Beyond the field, there'd be a stretch of wooded hills and gullies hiding the old state highway that nobody used anymore because of the interstate, and beyond that the strip pits, filled with black water, and the silent, boarded-up mine buildings.

In that moment, I felt more like an outsider than I had since I'd first arrived. I'd been grateful then for the chance to keep on being a cop, instead of winding up guarding some factory or shopping mall, or maybe sneaking around hotel lobbies taking pictures of errant spouses. Now I wasn't as sure as I'd once been. Maybe because my father had been a cop, I'd always just assumed that being a cop meant being the good guy. Until I'd become one myself. It struck me how ironic it was that one of the hardest things to hold on to, sometimes, when you're a cop, is the conviction that you're the good guy and the other guys are the bad guys. Either that or, like Bullard, you start thinking that everyone who isn't a cop is some kind of bad guy—and maybe some of the cops as well.

Behind me, I heard the bathroom door open. Marcie's steps went toward the living room, then back toward me, and she came into the kitchen. She wasn't smiling, but she'd clearly gotten on top of it. She lifted some old newspapers off a stool in one corner and sat down, hooking her bare toes on the rungs. I waited for her to speak.

After a moment, she said, "Eddie was a . . . little, scared, underweight kid. He always wanted the other guys to like him, to let him hang around, so he went along with them. That was always his problem. When he was little, he used to give away his favorite toys to kids he wanted to be friends with. It never worked."

I didn't say anything. She bit her lower lip and looked up at a corner of the ceiling, as though studying something there.

"What you don't understand," she said at last, "is how scared he was of going back to prison. Things happened to him in there." She looked straight at me for the first time. "Sexual things."

"I didn't know that," I said, though I supposed I could have guessed. That was one of the things it didn't pay to think about too much if you were a cop, if you had to send people up.

"Of course he wouldn't tell you," Marcie said bitterly. "You were one of the tough guys he wanted to like him. He couldn't even tell me directly, just kind of hinted at it. And he cried. . . ." She stopped, tears running down her own cheeks. "That's how I knew," she said at last, ignoring the tears.

"I did like Eddie," I said.

She looked at me and her face softened slightly. "I know," she said. "But that's why he killed himself. Not because he was guilty. I want you to understand that. He wasn't guilty."

I sighed, unable to look at her. "I don't like to think so, either," I said. "Last night, I was sure. . . . " I shook my head. "He's still the best suspect," I said. "The only suspect. That's what it comes down to. He was there, and he ran, and he had the money on him."

"He told you about the money. And he ran because he knew he'd be blamed. He knew how things work around here."

"What do you mean?"

She gave me a harsh, pitying look that made me feel small and stupid. "Somebody on Circle Street gets killed," she said, "and someone from Randall Drive is right there. Are the Elk Rapids police going to look any further than that for a suspect?"

"If there was evidence," I said.

"How hard did they look for evidence, once they'd picked up Eddie?" she asked.

I started to answer her, then realized I couldn't. That had been the point at which I'd disqualified myself. I'd glanced at the reports from the crime scene, but I hadn't really studied them. And I hadn't supervised that part of the investigation. Mike had—an old cop who maybe just wanted everything to go smoothly for this last two months. It annoyed me how that thought kept popping up.

"I know it wasn't you, Johnny," she said. "I know you thought you were doing the right thing, letting the others handle it, but it might have been better for Eddie if you'd been the one. You haven't been around here long enough to know how it's supposed to work."

"And how's that?" I asked.

She shrugged. "If they don't know who really did something, someone from Randall Drive will always do. In their minds, that makes everything even again. Over here, you know, we're just trash, disposable. It doesn't really matter whether Eddie did it or not. Somebody has to pay. He'll do." Her voice had grown soft, reflective, as though she were talking to herself.

"I haven't seen anything like that," I said. "Pat Bullard's from Kansas City, just like I am, and he's a good cop."

"You see what you want to see," she said, her voice sharp again. "And down here, being a good cop means you kiss the right asses and do what you're told. Your chief's been tight with Dexter and his buddies since about ten minutes after he got here. Maybe since before that, for all I know."

I shrugged. "You have to deal with the power structure anywhere, Marcie," I said. "Even in Kansas City."

She gave me a twisted smile. "So 'good cop' means the same thing everywhere," she said.

"That's not fair," I said.

She turned away, swiveling on the stool. After a long moment of silence, she turned back and said, "What did you mean about last night? You started to say something."

I hesitated, reluctant to get into it. "I went and saw Eddie," I said. "I was just checking in on him, that's all. He was in pretty good spirits. He was talking about different options, copping a plea, not copping a plea and taking his chances, that kind of thing. And . . . he sounded like he wanted to talk about what actually happened, what he knew. But he was afraid of that, for some reason—more afraid of that than of going to prison, I thought, but from what you say I guess I was wrong." I paused and thought about that. Something came together. Why had Eddie posed his hypothetical question in terms of a husband and wife—a husband who made the wife do things she didn't want to do? Could Elmore have been an old queer, Eddie his lover, perhaps not quite voluntarily? Elmore's reclusiveness fit, as did his hidden past, his lack of a real social life. And now what Marcie had said made Eddie fit as well. Sometimes, I knew, guys found out in prison that they were gay. Or maybe it turned them gay. I wasn't sure how that worked. Some guys could go either way. And some guys liked it and some guys couldn't live with it. Maybe Eddie had been one of those. Marcie said he'd cried when he'd tried to tell her what had happened to him in prison. Maybe that's why the idea of having to tell

49

exactly what had happened had bothered him more than confessing to the crime itself.

"What are you thinking?" Marcie asked.

I looked at her, stuck for an answer. Maybe I could suggest this line of thought to her sometime, as a way of getting her to accept what had happened, but now wasn't the time. It wouldn't do her any good. It certainly wouldn't help exonerate him. It only made his guilt seem more likely.

"Nothing," I lied. "Something last night gave me the idea that Eddie might be protecting someone, but I don't see who it could be, or why he'd kill himself if that were the case."

That seemed to interest her. Her eyes slid away from mine, toward the window above the sink. After a moment she looked back at me and asked, "What are you going to do about it?"

"Nothing," I said. "There's nothing to do about it. It isn't even my case."

"So you're just going to go along with the rest of them."

"Marcie, that's all I can do. Whether you think he did it or not, or even whether I think so—that's not evidence. It doesn't give us anything to work with. All the evidence there is still points to Eddie."

"Maybe," she said, then gave me an intense look and said, "You don't believe he did it, do you, Johnny?"

There was a plea in the question, and I thought hard about it before answering. I knew it was important to her—to us. But the more I thought about it, the more the homosexual angle seemed to answer all the questions, to make everything fit, even the suicide.

"I hate thinking he did it, Marcie," I said at last. "But . . ." I shook my head. "If you put me on the stand and made me swear, I'd have to say, yes, I think he probably did it. I wish it weren't so."

We looked at each other for a moment, then she looked

away and said, "Then I don't need you anymore. I don't have any use for you."

I stood there for a moment, wanting to find something to say, wanting her to look at me, but I didn't and she wouldn't, and after a while I walked out of the kitchen and through the house and got back in my car and drove away.

CHAPTER
SIX

It wasn't lunchtime yet and I didn't feel like going back to the station, so I drove downtown to the newspaper building.

Rob Lucas had an office on the third floor. His father had bought the newspaper during the Depression, when the previous owner had gone bankrupt, and after college Rob had worked there, working his way up quickly, the way the boss's son will, to business manager and then to publisher when his father died.

His secretary smiled at my badge and picked up a sleek phone receiver. "There's an Officer Branch to see you," she said. After a moment, she said, "Yes, sir," and hung up. She smiled almost as sweetly at me as she had at my badge. "Mr. Lucas is with someone just now," she said, "but if you'd care to wait he should be free in a few minutes."

I sat down in one of the wooden armchairs. She went back to her word processor.

Pretty soon the inner office door opened and a heavyset guy in a red vest, carrying a tan raincoat over his arm, came out with Lucas right behind him. They shook hands. Lucas was smiling, but the other guy didn't seem too happy. He gave me a glance and then went out through the glass door.

"Come on in, lieutenant," Lucas said. There was a thin bandage on his forehead.

"That was Dan Mikulski, wasn't it?" I asked when we were sitting. Mikulski was the county chairman of Lucas's party.

Lucas nodded, giving a wry smile.

"I try not to conduct any campaign business in this office," he said. "I try to keep that separate. But it's hard to get that across to the old guys. Dan probably spent more time in here than I have, when my father was alive."

"You tell him about the accident?"

"Yes. I figured it'll come out one way or another."

"Surely it won't be in the newspaper," I said.

"It might," he said, with just a touch of impatience. "I don't tell them what to print. I'm not that kind of publisher, even when I'm not running for office. I worked in the newsroom for a while and I respect what they do. More than my father did, if you want to know the truth. I just handle the business part of things. Charlie MacIver runs the newsroom."

"But when it comes down to it, he works for you."

"That's true," Lucas said. "But I started out working for him, as a kid reporter, covering blue-ribbon winners at the county fair. I'm not sure he realizes anything has changed since then." Lucas gave a happy smile, as though that suited him just fine. I found myself starting to like him. I could see why people would vote for him.

"So how are you feeling now?" I asked.

"Better than I did yesterday. When I woke up, my head felt about two sizes too large and my tongue tasted like the bottom of a rug."

"It wasn't the accident that caused that," I said.

He looked at me speculatively, not saying anything. I fished in my jacket pocket and came up with the little medicine bottle I'd taken out of his glove compartment. I set it on the edge of his desk. He looked at it.

"It's empty," he said.

I nodded.

"You kept the pills," he said.

I nodded again.

Finally he shrugged and scooped up the bottle. "They're legal," he said. "You can check if you want. Dr. Blaine gives me a prescription and I get it filled at his clinic. My insurance even covers it. They're for my headaches. Without them I can't function. I have to lie around all day with the lights off and a washrag over my eyes. The slightest sound is like an ice pick in my skull."

"Funny the bottle's unlabeled," I said.

"Not really. I get them in large bottles and then put a few in this bottle to carry around with me."

"Are you hooked?" I asked.

He blinked and was silent for a moment. I had the impression he was really thinking about it, and that it was something he'd thought about before. "I need them," he said slowly. "I take them regularly, to prevent the headaches. I don't know whether I'd have any trouble quitting them, but I don't expect to have to." It sounded like something he'd recited before, maybe to himself.

"They weren't doing you any good last night," I said.

He picked up a paper clip from the desk top, partly straightened it, and began cleaning his fingernails with it. After a moment he said, "Even if the pills are bad for me in some way, they're better than the headaches. And the pills really had very little to do with what happened last night. That was simply . . . a relapse."

"What kind of relapse?"

He gave a heavy sigh and put the paper clip down. "Is there a purpose to this interrogation?" he asked. "Is there a problem about the accident?"

"No," I said. "Just professional curiosity, I guess. The car's at the county lot. You can have it taken somewhere to be worked on. There'll probably be a towing and storage charge."

"Thanks for taking care of it. Thanks for everything. I really do appreciate it."

"What about the girl?" I asked.

His expression turned gloomy and he swiveled and looked out the window behind him. Main Street ran off toward the Elk River Bridge and you could see the strip of brown water and the hills on the other side, beyond the edge of town. The river ran slightly downhill, the water gurgling over round rocks. It wasn't what a white-water kayaker would call rapids—you could wade in it without getting your shorts wet— but it had given the town its name. It occurred to me that Rob's office window probably offered the most scenic view you could find in Elk Rapids.

"She was gone when I woke up," he said. "I guess Clare took care of her."

"I get the impression she takes care of a lot of things," I said.

"Yes." He swiveled back to look at me again. "She's always been the kind to take charge of things, ever since we were small. Our mother died when I was born, and Clare . . . well, Clare sort of raised me, even though she's only three years older than me." He shrugged. "But Clare doesn't do anything she doesn't want to do," he said. "She doesn't do anything without a good reason." He gave me a bright smile that seemed somehow an attempt to deny what he'd just said.

"You grew up in the house on Circle Street?" I asked.

He nodded. "My father bought it around the same time he bought the newspaper. There were lots of bargains to be had during the Depression." There was just a trace of bitterness in his voice.

"And most of your neighbors have probably lived there just as long," I said.

"Longer," he said. "Most of our neighbors live in houses their great-grandparents built, back in the coal mining days."

"So I guess when someone new moves in, it must be quite

55

an event," I said. "People talk about it more than they would in a normal neighborhood."

He smiled. "I always thought it was a normal neighborhood," he said. "I suppose everyone feels that way about the place where he grew up. But I know what you mean. You're talking about Elmore? When he moved in?"

I nodded. Lucas was a bit sharper than I'd been giving him credit for. "You heard about Eddie Skubitz," I said.

"We're running it on page one this afternoon."

I had a brief image of Marcie going out to the front porch and unwrapping her paper, then put that thought aside.

"When a case ends this way," I said, "when the main suspect dies and it never goes to court, even when you're pretty sure you got the right guy, it leaves a lot of unanswered questions. It leaves an unfinished feeling."

"I can understand that," Lucas said.

"Most of the unanswered questions in this case have to do with Elmore," I said. "Understand: This isn't part of the investigation. This is just me, trying to satisfy myself."

He nodded. "I get it," he said. "Off the record." He smiled. "What is it you're after?"

"Just . . ." I shook my head. "Just anything about Elmore," I said. "Gossip, even. Hunches you may have had about him, or that other people may have had and passed on to you. Nobody seems to have known much about him. Surely there must have been some speculation. I'm trying to get a picture of him, of how people saw him."

Lucas sat back in his chair and steepled his hands, looking past me at the far wall. After a moment he shrugged. "I'm not sure I can help you," he said. "I already told the other detective everything I could think of. The only impression I had of Elmore was of a quiet, pleasant, middle-aged man who seemed to have enough investment income to live on and not much to do."

"Do you think that had always been the case?" I asked. "Or do you think he'd once had something to do?"

Lucas blinked and looked at me. "When you put it that way . . ." he said. "That's funny. For some reason, I do have an idea that he'd once worked in the financial area." He frowned. "I don't know exactly why. I guess it was the way he used certain words. Everyone in that . . . crowd knows something about investments—the men, anyway. It's one of the things they talk about a lot. You know. Sports, business . . . but . . . I can't give you a good example, but it's the way lawyers will use legal terms in conversation, as though they were just ordinary words. It seems to me Elmore used economic terms that way. Without really thinking about it, I guess I've always assumed he was a retired stockbroker or banker, maybe an insurance executive. Something in that area, anyway." He looked at me and gave a soft laugh, as if surprised by what he'd said.

"Try something else," I said. "What about his social life?"

He shook his head. "He went to some of the same parties I did," he said. "That's really all I know about that."

"That's not really what I mean," I said. "You said he talked a certain way about business, finances, that kind of thing. How did he talk about, say, women, for example?"

Lucas's face grew solemn, almost stern. "You mean when all the guys got together in the steam room at the country club and swapped dirty jokes?" he asked.

"Whatever," I said.

Lucas thought about it and his face gradually relaxed. "Well, now that you mention it," he said, "I'd have to say that Elmore had a rather . . . coarse sense of humor. A rather cynical view of women, I'd say." He gave a soft, humorless grunt of laughter. "In fact," he said, "I'd guess he didn't like women very much."

"Do you think he liked them at all?" I asked.

He started to smile, but then he looked at me a bit more closely.

"What exactly do you mean by that?" he asked.

"Well," I said, "it must have occurred to you. A single man that age, living by himself, having no known lady friends—that's pretty well established—spending a lot of time alone with a young man he'd essentially picked up at the county courthouse . . ."

"Yes, I see," Lucas said. "You know, the striking thing is that that hadn't occurred to me before, and I can't remember anyone ever suggesting it. That right there tells you something, doesn't it? What you're saying makes sense from where you sit, but I don't think anybody who knew Elmore at all would have thought he was anything but heterosexual. Rather coarsely so, as I said."

"It couldn't have been an act, a case of protesting too much?"

Lucas shrugged. "I suppose so, but if so it was a hell of an act. On the other hand, I didn't really know him all that well. And we never really know much about what goes on inside each other's lives, do we? I think we can all be thankful for that." He gave me a pointed look.

"This isn't just gossip," I said. "I'm not going to go around and chat with your neighbors about your driving and dating habits, or your medical problems."

Lucas's smile tightened. "It never entered my mind," he said.

I stood up. "Is there anyone you know of who was at all close to Elmore?" I asked.

He shook his head. "There were some people he spent a little more time with than others."

"Such as?"

He thought a moment. "Well, I'm pretty sure Elmore bought all his clothes at Harrison's, down the block, and I'd see him and Lowell Harrison together sometimes, at the country club, at parties, that kind of thing. They were about the same age. But Lowell's not exactly what I'd call . . . perceptive. And I doubt that Elmore was pouring his heart out to him." He shrugged.

"Thanks," I said. "I appreciate your time."

"Not at all." He stood and gave me his hand across the desk. I shook it.

Lowell Harrison was a slightly pompous man. Or maybe it was just that he sensed I wasn't a likely customer. The suit he wore was a good advertisement for his shop, though, because you had to look closely to see that he had quite a little beer belly on him. I knew after I'd talked to him for five minutes that he wasn't going to tell me anything useful about Elmore.

"I don't see what the point of your questions is, officer," he said. "Bill Elmore was simply a decent, respectable man who was savagely murdered by one of those hooligans from the south end of town. I don't see that there's any great mystery about it. He led a quiet life, valued his privacy. Nothing remarkable in that, and I don't see why his privacy should be invaded any further now. As far as I'm concerned, the killer saved everyone a lot of trouble by killing himself, and it seems to me the police ought to be getting on to other matters now." He lifted his chin slightly, obviously pleased with his little speech, and waited for me to skulk away, abashed.

"I'm just trying to clear up a few loose ends," I said. "A murder case is never officially closed if there isn't a conviction."

"Well, surely there's no doubt in this case, though."

"Why do you say that? Did you have some reason to suspect Eddie Skubitz? Did you know him?"

"Certainly not. Never met him. But I know the sort. You see them on the street corners, driving around in their trashy pickup trucks, or on their motorcycles. Pretending to be respectful and then grinning at decent people behind their backs. They're worthless people. Bill Elmore wasn't from around here, so he didn't know. He made the mistake of taking one of them in, trying to treat him decently, and you see what happened."

"Did you try to warn him?" I asked. Despite my best efforts, a trace of sarcasm crept into the words, but Harrison didn't appear to notice.

"None of my business," he said. "Perhaps I should have. I did try to discourage him from spending quite so much on the suit, though, even though it was money out of my pocket."

"What suit?"

"The suit of clothes he was going to buy for the boy. He said he'd go as high as three hundred dollars, and I told him that was far too much for a boy of that sort. Sport coat and slacks. That's all he'd ever really need. Probably find something quite suitable at K mart, actually." Harrison shrugged, a faint look of distaste on his face, as if he'd noticed some distant, disagreeable odor. "I got him down to two hundred dollars, but I couldn't persuade him to handle it on his account. He said he was going to give the boy the money, let him pretend he was buying it himself. I knew that was asking for trouble. Probably what caused . . ."

"When did he tell you that?" I asked.

"The day before he was murdered. That afternoon. The boy was supposed to show up the next morning, but of course he never did. Once he got the money, he took it and ran, just as I would have expected."

"Have you told anyone about this?" I asked.

He blinked at me in surprise. "About what?"

"Elmore telling you he was giving Eddie Skubitz two hundred dollars to buy a suit."

He shrugged. "Not that I recall. No one ever asked me about it. It never came up." He frowned, beginning to realize he might have said something important. "Why?"

"If Elmore gave him the money," I said, "why should Eddie bother to kill him?"

"Why . . ." Harrison spluttered, apparently astonished

by the question. ''Because he was a vicious little beast, obviously. I suppose he thought there was more money to be had.''

''Maybe you're right,'' I said. ''I wonder why he didn't look for it before he ran.''

Harrison started to splutter again, but I turned and left the shop. When I paused outside the door and glanced back, I saw Harrison watching me with a dark, suspicious look, his forehead furrowed in unaccustomed concentration.

I went back to the station, but Mike wasn't around. I left him a note, summarizing what Harrison had told me, then went out and had some lunch. If Marcie had been there to ask me again whether I thought Eddie had done it or not, I honestly wouldn't have known what to say. Harrison corroborated Eddie's story about the two hundred dollars, which took away the official motive, and Lucas had thrown cold water on the other possible motive I'd been working on. But that still didn't rule it out. I'd met too many people who were absolutely dumbfounded to learn that the nice man in the next apartment was a crack dealer, or a neo-Nazi nut with a sizable arsenal in his closet. It was quite possible that Elmore could have had everyone completely fooled about his sexual preferences. Terry Gardens had had me completely fooled, right up until the moment she put me straight herself with a few well-chosen words, and I'd been a lot closer to her than anyone around here had been to Bill Elmore.

On balance, though, it seemed to me that everything I'd learned was in Eddie's favor, which should have made me feel better, but only made me feel worse. Because it was too late. No matter what I found out now, Eddie was dead and he'd stay that way. If I wound up clearing him—which I was still a long way from doing—it might make Marcie feel better eventually, maybe even feel better about me, but it wasn't going to do much for how she felt about Eddie right now. It was just going to make her wonder, as I was wondering, why someone couldn't have asked Lowell Harrison the right question a day sooner. Meanwhile, I had my own job to do.

As it turned out, in fact, I didn't see Mike that afternoon, as I'd planned, because I got tied up with a neighborhood dispute—a dog had died and the owners were sure it had been poisoned, and then someone had fired shots at the front porch of the alleged poisoner's house. By the time I'd satisfied myself that things weren't going to escalate any further—mostly with a lot of threats to both sides—it was supper time and the dispatcher told me Mike had gone home. There was no message for me, but the note I'd left wasn't on his desk anymore.

I thought maybe it was time I had a word with Bullard about the things that were starting to bother me, but he wasn't in his office. The dispatcher told me he'd gone 10–7 at the Blue Tattoo a half hour before.

The Blue Tattoo was a private supper club on the grounds of the truck stop complex. When they wrote the Kansas Constitution, they stuck in a simple, straightforward clause: There shall be no open saloons in the state of Kansas. Then they spent a century or so arguing about what that meant and trying to get out from under it. One of the results was the "private club"—a members-only restaurant and bar, where you could buy liquor by the drink. In theory, the members could only buy setups, and had to add their own booze. But the clubs had evolved gradually to the point where, instead of bringing their own bottles, members paid periodically into a liquor pool, and the club used that money to stock the bar. The club—again in theory—made no profit on the liquor, which kept food prices high. Then, a couple of years ago, after several false starts, the voters of the state had okayed a constitutional amendment to make liquor by the drink a local option. Jacobson County was one of the few in the eastern half of the state that hadn't jumped at the opportunity. Consequently, local people who wanted to buy a drink with their meal had to belong to a club like the Blue Tattoo or drive over to one of the adjoining counties.

I'd been told that the name Blue Tattoo was a kind of joke left over from the coal mining days—something to do with the way a miner's skin would absorb coal dust over the years, finally forming a dark, visible pattern on the skin, often on the side of the head. It didn't seem very funny to me, but in those days it had mostly been the mine owners and their friends who had frequented the Blue Tattoo, and maybe they had gotten a chuckle out of it. Those old boys had all had names like Collins and Johnson and Lucas, and you could still find those names over on Circle Street. The mine workers had mostly had names like Sadowsky and Gennaro and Skubitz, and—apart from the ones like Dexter who had moved to the other side of town—you could still find those names out on Randall Drive. The mines were long closed, but they had left a dark tattoo on the social structure of the city. Now that I thought about it, maybe there was something funny about the name, with someone like Dexter owning the place where the mine owners had once gathered, after they had long since gone bust and found other lines of work or simply disappeared. The Blue Tattoo was now decorated with old lanterns and picks and framed photos of grimy miners, grinning for posterity—remnants of a dead era—and I was pretty sure that that hadn't been the decor in the old days.

Bullard's car was in the lot outside, but I didn't see him either in the public restaurant, where you couldn't buy a drink, or in the private part, where you could if you were a member. He wasn't in the bar, either. I stopped there and ordered a beer, asking the bartender if he'd seen the chief.

"Probably up with Dexter," he said, nodding toward the ceiling.

Dexter had converted the upper floor of the place into a large, lavish apartment, where he lived. The legend was that that floor had once been an exclusive brothel for the upper crust of Elk Rapids. He had his main offices over at the truck stop, but he maintained a small office here, where he could usually be found in the evenings. Once a month or so, Dexter had a Las Vegas night—invitation only—up at his place, with imported slots and tables. It was technically illegal, but according to Bullard—who was often on the guest list—Dexter actually made no profit on it. He took enough from the house winnings to pay for the equipment and staff, and then divided the rest among those who attended, crediting it to their accounts at the Blue Tattoo. So it mostly amounted to a bunch of old rich guys finding a complicated way to swap their money around for an evening. After the stuff I'd seen in Kansas City, it didn't seem any more serious to me than a bingo game—which was also illegal in Kansas, except for churches.

I finished my beer and went out to the foyer and up the stairs to the second floor. At the top, I was confronted by a slender guy with a neat mustache, dressed in an expensive charcoal-gray suit and a pink tie. His shirt was also gray, a lighter shade than the suit, and his hair looked razor cut, his fingers manicured. Dexter usually had a flunky around somewhere, but this was something new.

"Can I help you?" he asked politely, casually blocking the narrow hallway with his body. From the hang of his coat, it didn't look like he had a gun. Nor did he look particularly strong, although slender guys can fool you that way. I wondered how he planned to stop me if I just went on by.

"I'm Lieutenant Branch," I said. "Elk Rapids Police. I'm looking for Chief Bullard. I was told he might be with Dexter."

The man didn't appear overly impressed. He gave me an impassive once-over, then said, "Wait here. I'll check." I had seen that attitude before, in Kansas City; it was the attitude of someone who assumes you're on the take, just another employee of the big guys. For a moment something burned down inside me, but I squelched it. Checking my anger, or just about any strong emotion that might lead to it, had become a reflex during the last two years, since the night I'd let it get away from me, in Doolie Waters's apartment.

The man with the mustache reappeared and nodded to me to go ahead. He walked behind me down the hallway, then opened the door for me. Dexter was sitting in his swivel chair, his shoeless feet up on the desk. Bullard sat in an armchair in the corner, his tie pulled loose. Both of them had drinks in their hands. Dexter waved at me to come on in, and my escort closed the door and disappeared silently.

"Where'd he come from?" I asked, nodding at the door.

"Nick? He's a distant relative. Nephew of a cousin, something like that." He shrugged, as though unclear about it himself. "Needed a job, so I'm helping out."

"That's nice," I said. "Where's he from?"

"Back east." He waved vaguely to one side—actually more north than east—and said, "Make yourself a drink."

There was a little bar against the wall on one side, next to a second doorway that led into Dexter's living quarters. I opened the little cubical refrigerator and found a beer, then went and sat on the sofa opposite the desk.

"He said you were looking for me," Bullard said. He looked relaxed and content, a way I'd never seen him look on the job. His useless right arm was lying motionless on the arm of his chair, palm up, as though he expected somebody to hand him something, perhaps a bowl of nuts.

I nodded. "I wanted to talk to you about the Elmore thing," I said.

His face darkened slightly and he glanced at Dexter, who was sitting back, smiling his pleasant avuncular smile.

"If it's business, you ought to save it for the office," Bullard said.

"I know," I said. "It's just been eating at me."

"You gotta learn to leave the job at the office," Bullard said. "Ain't that right, Dexter?"

Dexter nodded agreeably.

"I found out something," I said.

Bullard sighed. "What?"

"Eddie Skubitz was telling the truth about Elmore giving him the two hundred dollars for a suit. Lowell Harrison confirms it."

Bullard frowned.

"You passed that on to Mike?" he asked after a moment.

"He wasn't around. I left him a note."

Bullard nodded. "Fine," he said. "You've done what you're supposed to. Now Mike will do his job. What's the problem?"

I rolled the cool beer can between my hands for a moment, thinking about how to approach it. "If we'd found this out sooner," I said at last, "Eddie Skubitz would probably still be alive."

Bullard shrugged. "If the FBI had known about Oswald, Kennedy'd still be alive," he said. "So what?"

"Well . . . for one thing, I feel like it's partly my fault. For taking myself off the case."

Bullard gave a grunt of laughter. "You don't think much of yourself, do you? What makes you think you'd have come up with it any sooner?"

"Well," I said, finally getting down to it, "I'm not getting ready to retire in two months."

The silence in the room told me I hadn't been quite as subtle as I'd hoped. Dexter swiveled slightly away from us and studied his glass, looking embarrassed.

"You come up here," Bullard said at last, "when I'm with a friend, off duty, to make an accusation against another officer?" His eyes were cold with amazement.

"It's not like that," I said, wanting to back up and start over. "I like Mike. I respect him. I hate to think of him finishing up badly. But . . . I don't feel good about the way this investigation has gone. I just wanted to talk to you about it."

"You think someone else should take over the case?" Bullard asked, his voice deceptively reasonable.

"I don't know. Maybe . . . ."

"Maybe you?" he asked. "Is that what you're saying? You want me to pull him off it, give it back to you?"

"I didn't say . . ."

"I won't do that to him," he said sharply. "You had your chance and you backed away, for your own reasons. Okay. Now let it lie. Mike Farrar has been a cop longer than you've been alive. He's been a detective for twenty-five years. He's had seven citations for bravery. He's been wounded twice. He's my chief of detectives, and that's not just 'cause I like him. It's 'cause he's good. And this is his case now and I trust him to do it right, no matter how many little pissant hoodlums hang themselves. You got that?"

I stared at him, feeling a responsive flare of anger deep down inside me, but ignoring it. "Yes," I said. "I understand that. But what if . . . ?"

"What if shit. I got nothing more to say about this." Bullard set his empty glass down on the floor and stood up. "You got anything else to say to me, you say it in my office, not in front of outsiders. No offense, Dexter."

Dexter waved his glass genially, dismissing the remark. Bullard gave him a nod and went out, closing the door behind him.

I sat back and took a drink of the beer. "Well," I said, "I fucked that up."

"Yes," Dexter said sympathetically, "I'm afraid you did."

"He misunderstood what I was saying," I said.

"I'm sure he did," Dexter said diplomatically. "But you have to realize that loyalty is very important to Pat, especially within his own organization. He feels he was betrayed by his former colleagues, in Kansas City. You understand that?"

I nodded. I understood it all too well.

"You just pushed the wrong button," Dexter said.

"I'll straighten it out with him," I said. I got up and put

67

the empty beer can in the wastebasket beside his desk. "Sorry to break things up here," I said.

Dexter waved a hand. "Don't worry about me," he said. "I just hate to see you causing problems for yourself, when you could so easily write your own ticket here."

I stopped and looked at him. "What do you mean?"

"Oh, just that Pat thinks a lot of you. So do the rest of us, for that matter. But we don't see much of you. You seem to keep your distance. And then something like this happens." He shrugged. "Perspective," he said. "That's what it amounts to. Perspective. The difference between how you see things and how Pat sees things. You follow me?" He was looking at me more closely than before. "I don't have anything against the Skubitz girl," he said. "If I didn't think she was an honest, hard-working girl, I wouldn't have her working at the coffee shop. I have nothing against your . . . friendship with her. But . . . well, all I'm saying is that you've been in Elk Rapids two years now, and who do you really know besides her? Maybe it's time you thought about broadening your circle of friends, gaining some perspective, becoming more a part of the community. The part of the community that really counts, I mean. It might help you get along with Pat, see things more from his point of view. He has a job to do here, too, you know."

"I know," I said. There was a part of me that didn't like what he was saying, but there was another part that felt he might be right and was a little embarrassed about it. I had had a shell around me ever since Kansas City. I'd made myself an outsider there, and it was as if I felt I didn't deserve to be anything else here. Marcie had been my only real contact, as Dexter said, and she was an outsider, too, in her own way. Perspective, I thought, wondering how much of my suspicion of Mike was just the outsider's paranoia, multiplied by my concern for Marcie, my absorption of her own paranoia about the way things worked in Elk Rapids. The fact was, I had no reason to think that Mike had been doing anything but his best on the Elmore case. It wasn't his fault Eddie had killed himself.

"You think about what I said," Dexter said. He was giving me his look of concern.

"I will," I said. "I am." I went out and back down the stairs. Nick was leaning against the bar and he gave me a nod and tiny smile as I went past, as if he knew all about what had happened upstairs.

CHAPTER
SEVEN

I felt even more like a horse's ass the next morning, when Mike came into my office and flopped down in the chair in front of my desk.

"I feel awful about the kid," he said. "We should have found out about that money earlier."

The night before, I'd been prepared to question his professionalism. Now I found that all I wanted to do was reassure him.

"I only found out by accident," I said. "Harrison didn't realize it was important."

"Still . . ." He shook his head sadly.

"What are you going to do?"

"I'm stuck," he said. "Without the two hundred dollars, we got no motive for the kid, and after the stuff he told you, I'm inclined to doubt he did it, anyway. But I haven't got idea one about what direction to look next."

I told him what Marcie had told me, about what had happened to Eddie in prison, and how it seemed to me to fit with the things Eddie had said—his reluctance to talk about the details of what had happened, the nature of the hypothetical situation he'd made up—and with what little we knew of Elmore.

"It also makes the suicide easier to explain," I said.

Mike was nodding his head, his gaze turned inward. "Yeah, I see what you mean," he said. "But we don't know anything like that was really going on. None of Elmore's friends suggested anything like that."

"I know. I sounded out Rob Lucas about it, and he didn't buy it at all. But how many practicing gays do these folks around here know? Elmore had a lifetime to develop his protective coloring."

Mike pursed his lips, looking skeptical but not quite as whipped as he had a moment before. "It's something to look into," he said. "I'd like to get this settled, one way or the other, before I leave."

"And if it turns out I'm wrong . . ." I said.

"Then most likely there's still a killer out there somewhere."

There was a little silence and then I said, "Mike, I hope you don't resent my getting involved the way I have, talking to Lucas and Harrison."

He blinked and shook his head. "No, no," he said. "I can use all the help I can get." He gave a little smile. "Anyway," he said, "it's because of the girl, isn't it?"

I felt myself begin to blush and had to look away, embarrassed more by what I'd been thinking about him than by what he'd said. "I just want you to know," I said, "that if you want me to stay out of it, I will. Just say the word."

He stared at me for a long time, apparently taking the offer seriously, then said, "If Eddie didn't do it, and if I don't figure out who did do it in the next two months, it'll be your case again anyway. Might as well keep close to it. Just let me know anything you find out."

So I did some more checking around over the next couple of days, but I couldn't come up with a whiff of anything that suggested Elmore might have been gay. In one way, I was glad, because it took Eddie off the hook; in another way, I wasn't, because it put Mike back on. It was becoming obvious that I wasn't going to end up feeling good about this case, no matter how it came out.

The third night after I'd talked to Eddie, I was driving, listening to an oldies tape, when I caught something on the two-way.

I grabbed the mike and said, "This is twenty-two. Ten–nine that last transmission."

"Security Services Inc. reports a code 16 at Eleven Circle Street," the dispatcher repeated. Code 16 was a burglar alarm going off, most likely a silent alarm that tripped a light on the security company console. Eleven Circle Street was the Elmore house.

"I'll be enroute," I said. "Tell them to hold off until I get there, just watch for anybody coming out."

"Ten–four, twenty-two."

Five minutes later I was parking across the street from the house. There were lights in some of the other houses, including the Lucas place, two doors away, but no one seemed to have noticed the squad car parked in the Elmore drive. It was a hot, still night, with a distant pleasant smell in the air of something burning. Getting out of my car, I reflected that, if I'd smelled the same thing in Kansas City, where open burning is illegal, I'd have had it checked out. Here it was normal. Willis Seba, a young uniformed officer, met me at the sidewalk.

"Anything?" I asked.

He shook his head. "Might be a false alarm. Fred went around back to watch the door there."

"Okay. Let's check the front."

The door was locked. We went along the front of the house, checking window latches, Seba holding his flashlight up. We'd gotten nearly to the corner when we heard a short, sharp scream from around in back, followed by a male voice shouting something unintelligible.

I drew my revolver and motioned Seba to go the long way around, then went around the corner to the side yard. As I neared the back, I saw a faint glow. I peeked around the corner of the house and saw Fred Bechtold, Seba's partner, standing a few feet out into the yard, with his gun and flashlight both pointed toward the back of the house, where someone was flattened against the wall. It took me a moment to realize that it was a girl, but I couldn't see her face in the dark. She dropped something that made a thunk in the grass, and I stepped out into the yard and shone my own light on it. It was one of those cheap little flashlights that you turn on by twisting the cap, the kind women keep in their purses. The girl turned and looked at me. It was Marcie.

She closed her eyes and turned her head away. She had one arm pressed tightly across her waist, and the other hand clutched at the shingled wall behind her, as though seeking a grip there. She was wearing a dark sweatshirt and blue jeans, both of which had smears of dust on them.

"She came up through the basement window," Bechtold said. "Scared the shit out of me."

"Sounded like you scared each other," I said.

At my voice, Marcie turned toward me again, her face tense, guarded.

"What are you doing here?" I asked her.

"What you ought to be doing," she said. Her voice came through clenched teeth.

"Find anything?" I asked.

She shook her head sullenly, staring down at her feet.

"Shit," I said. "What am I gonna do with you now? Breaking and entering, for Christ's sake." I gave Bechtold a disgusted look. He'd started to grin, but wiped the grin off his face when I looked at him. "Take her to the car," I told him. "I'll be along in a minute."

He holstered his gun and went and put a hand on her arm. She turned passively to go with him, but kept her other arm clenched tight across her stomach.

"Wait a minute," I said.

They stopped. Bechtold looked at me, but Marcie stopped

with her back to me, her shoulders slightly hunched. I moved around in front of her.

"Take your arm away," I told her.

She didn't move, just kept staring stubbornly at the ground. I took hold of the arm and she squirmed violently, trying to twist away from me.

"What have you got?" I said.

In answer, she kicked out at me suddenly. I was quick enough to pivot and catch it on the side of my thigh, but it still hurt. The old anger flared suddenly and I slapped her across the face, then grabbed the arm and twisted it behind her. She gave a sharp gasp of pain and doubled over slightly. With my free hand I felt along her waistline until I came to something hard and flat pinned beneath the elastic of her jeans. She still tried to struggle away from me, but I managed to get my hands under the waistband and tug the object loose. It fell to the ground in front of her. I pulled her back away from it and Seba, who had come up from the other direction, shone his light on it. She stopped struggling and began crying softly. I let go of her arm, feeling chilled and a bit dizzy.

"What is it?" I said, my voice hoarse.

"Looks like a compact." Seba leaned over and nudged it with the flashlight, trying to turn it over, and it popped open suddenly. Inside was a cracked mirror and a sheet of yellow paper, folded in quarters. Marcie was standing with both hands to her face, tears running silently down her cheeks.

"Whose is this?" I asked.

Her head came up. "Mine," she said. "It's mine."

I bent over and picked it up by one corner, retrieving the sheet of paper with my other hand. The compact was either gold or gold plated. Despite the cracked mirror, it looked fairly new. There were no initials on it. The piece of paper appeared to be one of those thin, yellow sheets they call second sheets, used for making carbons, although nobody much made carbons anymore, what with computers. When I unfolded it, I found it had a simple map drawn on it in

74

pencil—the outline of two buildings, with doors and stairways crudely marked. There were two X's, one in the space between the two buildings, the other inside the larger building, at one edge. I studied it a moment, then looked around me at the house and the detached two-car garage. I showed it to Seba and his partner.

"That could be these buildings," I said. "Where would this X be?"

We went around the side of the house, nearest the garage, herding Marcie in front of us. She was completely passive now, all the fight gone out of her. She looked like a little kid again, in her dirty sweatshirt and jeans. She rubbed absentmindedly at the arm I'd twisted, making me feel guilty, but there didn't appear to be any bruise where I'd slapped her.

"Right in the middle of that flower bed," Bechtold said, pointing his flashlight.

The flower bed, it seemed to me, was in a funny place, in between the house and garage, out of sight of either the back or front yards, where the sun would have a hard time getting to it. Mostly it was full of some kind of leafy, ground-covering plant, with a few anemic blossoms poking up here and there. I stood and thought about everything for a few seconds, then looked at Marcie, who didn't look back.

"Where'd you get this map?" I asked her.

"I don't have to tell you anything," she said. "I'm supposed to have a lawyer."

I nodded.

"Take her to the car," I said. "Give her her rights and call for a female officer to accompany her in. Watch out she doesn't ditch anything on the way. Have her searched at the station."

"B and E?" Seba asked.

"Don't book her till I get there," I said. "Just hold her."

I went back across the street to my own car and got on the radio.

"I'll need an evidence team," I told the dispatcher. "And tell them to bring their shovels."

Back at the squad car, Marcie was sitting in the backseat, leaning against the far door, her face hidden in darkness. Bechtold leaned against the passenger door, his arms crossed, keeping an eye on her.

"I don't think she went in through that window," he said in a low voice.

"Why not?"

"They were all latched. I checked them. All the doors were locked, all the windows latched from the inside. She unlatched it to come out, but she must have gone in some other way."

"She could have latched it herself, once she was in," I said.

He frowned; it was something he hadn't thought of. "Why would she do that, though?" he said.

"I don't know," I said. "People do funny things when they're breaking the law and they aren't used to it."

"You really gonna book her?" he asked.

I shrugged. "I don't know," I said.

"She's really a nice girl," he said. "I knew her in high school."

"You grow up on that side of town, too?" I asked.

He shook his head. "Over on Commerce Street," he said. "It ain't Circle Street, but it ain't Randall Drive, either."

Seba came around the front of the house, his flashlight off.

"Lieutenant," he said, nearly whispering, "there's someone behind those bushes over there."

I looked. He meant the tall, square hedge that served as a fence between the Elmore place and the house next door.

"Probably the neighbors," I said.

"Maybe so, but they're keeping awful quiet. I went right by there, not three feet away, and I'd swear whoever it was stopped breathing."

I nodded. "Let's take a look. I'll go down the other side."

I went around the edge of the hedge, into the adjoining yard, and started along it. Before I'd gotten halfway up, Clarice Lucas stepped out of the darkness and stood looking at me, her head cocked slightly to one side.

"Good evening, detective," she said. "I heard a scream and thought I'd better take a look." A pistol dangled loosely in her right hand.

"Maybe you'd better let me have that," I said.

She shrugged, jacked the shell out of the chamber without looking at it, and handed me the gun butt first. It was a tiny, silver-plated automatic, with some kind of dark gemstones inlaid in the handle, almost a piece of jewelry. Someone had told me they were advertising guns like that these days, in *Vogue* and *Cosmopolitan*.

I handed it back, and she slipped it into the pocket of her robe. "Very pretty," I said.

She smiled. "It works."

"I'll bet it does. What did you have in mind?"

"I don't know. As I said, I heard the scream. I thought someone might need assistance."

"And then you saw all the cops here, and thought you better hang around in case we needed help subduing the girl," I said.

Her smile deepened. "I was curious," she said. "I admit it. Who is that girl, anyway?"

"Marcie Skubitz."

"Eddie's sister?"

"Yes."

"What was she doing?"

"That's what I hope to find out."

Headlights shone along the drive beyond the hedge.

"Lieutenant," Seba said from the other side.

"I have a feeling that once you've decided to find something out, you don't quit," Clarice said.

"Doggedness can sometimes take the place of intelligence," I said.

"That's true, but I doubt that it applies in this case."

"Why didn't Rob come?" I asked. "Afraid he'd find another body?'

Her smiled faded. "He hasn't come home yet," she said. "That's why I was still up."

"Another relapse, so soon?"

"I think there's something bothering him."

"Besides his wife, you mean?"

She nodded. "Probably just the campaign pressure."

"Or the headaches," I said.

She frowned at me.

"That he takes the pills for," I said.

"Oh." She shook her head. "It wouldn't be that. He doesn't worry about himself that way. In fact, he's a little reckless."

"I noticed," I said.

"But he cares about others," she said. "He really is a good man."

And Eddie really was a good kid, I thought. And Marcie really was a nice girl. I wondered how much sisters really knew about their brothers. Or vice versa. More than any of the rest of us knew about each other, I supposed.

"Try to get some sleep," I told her. "Rob will probably be okay, and I think we can muddle through here without you."

They didn't have to dig very far to find the body. It was wrapped in green plastic trash bags that had been torn apart along the creases, to make winding sheets. It had been there a long time; if it hadn't been wearing the remnants of a man's suit, we would have had trouble guessing the sex.

"Jesus," I said, "let's get it out of here. That smell's gonna be all over the neighborhood in a few minutes."

"Play hell with property values," Jack Molini said. He was the thin, bespectacled guy who ran the Elk Rapids police lab, such as it was. "Maybe I could afford a house here if we hung around long enough," he said.

"Anything besides the body?"

He nodded. "We may have gotten lucky. There's a briefcase with some papers inside that we might be able to salvage, and his wallet's still inside his jacket."

"Name?"

"I haven't looked in it. Didn't want to mess with it till I can get back to the lab."

"Let me know," I said. "I'll be around the station."

I found Marcie sitting in one of the interrogation rooms by herself, at the end of the long table, drinking a diet Coke out of a can. I looked at her through the one-way mirror before I went in. She was staring at the table in front of her, her expression sad but with something like resolve in it, too. The only thing they'd found on her had been a key, in one pocket of her jeans—a key to the Elmore house.

She looked up when I came in, and watched me expressionlessly as I sat down in the chair at the other end of the table.

"Where's the lawyer?" I asked.

"Do I really need one?"

"I guess that depends on the answers I get to some questions."

She gave an elaborate shrug that betrayed some nervousness, and waited.

"What did you expect to find at the Elmore place?" I asked.

"I didn't know. I wanted to see what the map led to."

"Where'd the map come from?"

"It was in the compact when I got it."

I sighed. "Okay, so where'd the compact come from?"

"Someone gave it to me."

"Who?" I asked as patiently as possible.

She shook her head.

"Was it Eddie?" I asked.

She shook her head again, harder, though I couldn't really tell if she meant it wasn't Eddie or that she just wasn't going to say. I let it pass for the moment.

"What about the key?" I asked.

She hesitated, then said, "Same place I got the compact and the map."

"The same person gave you all three."

She shrugged.

"I'm going to have to know who it was," I said.

"Then you're going to have to figure it out for yourself," she said.

"I could put you in a cell for a while and let you think about it."

She gave me a cold look of contempt. "You going to provide me with a length of rope, too?" she asked.

Anger washed over me. There was something in her look that reminded me of Terry Gardens at the moment when she'd finally told me, bluntly, how it really was between her and Doolie, and how it really was between her and me. That gave me an idea, something I hadn't thought of before.

"Was it Elmore who gave you the compact?" I asked.

Her face blanked with surprise, and she looked quickly away from me. In that instant, I knew I was right.

"You'd been seeing Elmore," I said, trying to keep the anger out of my voice. "That was why he was being so nice to your brother, wasn't it?" I remembered Eddie sitting in his cell, his earnest face behind the thick glasses, telling me his hypothetical story about a man who made a woman do things she didn't want to do, until she'd had enough and killed him, and me trying to figure out who he could have cared enough about to take the rap for.

Marcie was studying me, her eyes narrowed. "You think you've got it all figured out now?" she asked.

"Just about," I said. "But I'd like to know who that guy is who's buried in the flower bed."

"What?" Her surprise was either genuine or a terrific act.

"That's what the map led to," I said. "One of the X's, anyway. We're still looking for the other one. He was a man in a suit, with a briefcase. Nobody like that has been reported missing around here."

She sat in silence for a long time, her gaze turned inward. It looked like the news about the body had thrown her somehow, as if it were much different from what she'd expected. After a while she looked up at me and asked, "What about my compact? Do I get it back?"

I thought about it. First, I had to decide whether to hold her or not. There was no point in holding her for the break-in, but what about suspicion of murder? What did I have? A feeling that Eddie had been protecting someone. And the compact with the map and the key in it, along with her tacit admission that Elmore had given it to her. Plus my gut feeling that she was hiding something from me, the way Terry Gardens had hidden something from me. Was it anything more than an affair with Elmore? I wanted to be very careful this time around. Anyway, it wasn't my case. It felt like it was becoming important to remind myself of that. As for the compact, I'd checked the lists from the original search of the Elmore house, and it wasn't on them, which meant it hadn't been there, unless that search had been even sloppier than I feared. Anyway, I had recovered some of my faith in Mike's competence.

I took the compact out of my jacket pocket and slid it down the table toward her—perhaps a little harder than I'd intended, because it went off the end of the table. She caught it in her lap, knocking the can of Coke over as she did so. She set it upright again and looked around for something to wipe up the spill with.

"Leave it," I said. "This isn't the truck stop."

She gave me a hurt look, which surprised me.

"We're keeping the map and the key," I said. "I'm not

going to charge you with anything right now, but don't leave town. We may want to talk to you again.''

She licked her lips. ''Johnny . . .'' she said. She suddenly looked small and miserable.

Something rose in my throat, not anger so much as disappointment, a racking sense of loss, and I had to swallow hard. I didn't want to hear any confessions now.

I shook my head and stood up. ''I'll get someone to drive you home for now,'' I told her, and I went out of the room.

CHAPTER
EIGHT

Assuming the wallet in the jacket was his, the man buried in the flower bed was Lawrence Dixon, a bank clerk from Bethesda, Maryland. The Bethesda police had wired us a couple of photos which not surprisingly matched the photo on the driver's license in the wallet. The body itself was too far gone to match it with anything, visually, but we were looking into blood and teeth to confirm the ID.

We were pretty confident we'd confirm it, because two different employees at the Emerald Hotel had identified the photos as a "Mr. Johnson" who had checked in there for a couple of days, nine months earlier. They remembered him because he'd never checked out again, and they still had his suitcase. They'd reported the skipped hotel bill and the abandoned property, and someone in the department had looked into it, probably without much enthusiasm, and hadn't been able to trace him anywhere, except to establish that he'd arrived by bus from Wichita. He'd presumably flown into there, but there was no way to tell for sure. He hadn't been reported as a missing person, which wasn't surprising, since people really do skip out on hotel bills with some frequency, even occasionally leaving their luggage.

One of the doctors who worked with the coroner established that he'd been stabbed in the back with a long, thin knife, most likely a carving knife—perhaps even one of those hanging on the wall in the Elmore kitchen, though it was impossible to establish that. Would Elmore, assuming he killed Dixon, have washed the knife and hung it back on the wall, continued to use it? There didn't appear to be any missing from the set.

What was missing was whatever had been behind the furnace in the basement, at the spot marked by the other X on Marcie's map. You couldn't really tell there was any space back there at all unless you got on your hands and knees and crawled into the narrow gap between the furnace and the staircase—and apparently no one had done that during the first investigation, because no one had reported finding anything back there. Or maybe it had already been gone, and no one had thought anything about the vaguely rectangular clean place in the midst of dust that was half an inch thick. There were scuff marks where it had been dragged out, but there was no way of knowing how long ago that had been. From the way the dust settled, according to forensics, it could have been anywhere from a month to a few days. They were able to establish that it had been gone by the time Marcie showed up, but that was about it. Whether it had disappeared before or after Elmore's murder was impossible to tell. And of course we had no way of knowing what "it" was.

But that wasn't my problem. I was trying to figure out what to do about Marcie. My initial suspicion wasn't fading, as I'd hoped it might; it was settling in in the back of my mind like a nagging, unpleasant chore that remained to be done. And the fact that I hadn't said anything to Mike about it was also beginning to bother me. The fact was, I wasn't quite sure what I was doing or why; I kept telling myself to think like a cop, but it was as if I had somehow lost the knack. Maybe I had lost it in Kansas City, and was just now finding that out. Sometimes it seemed to me that I'd been wrong to release Marcie, but when I thought about the alternative—putting her into the same jail where her brother had killed himself—I knew I couldn't have done that, even if there hadn't been so many unanswered questions. I wasn't sure what to believe, about her or about myself, and it made me apprehensive, as though there were something just ahead that I would have to deal with but that I wasn't prepared for—and somehow it had the feel of unfinished business, like the reckoning I hadn't truly faced yet for what had happened in Kansas City. I was like a driver, driving in fog, knowing there's a crossroad somewhere just ahead and not knowing which way to go, not even knowing how near it is, or what it will look like.

I was sitting at my desk, staring at nothing, when Mike came in and put a couple of mug shots in front of me. One of them I didn't recognize.

"That's Dixon," Mike said, placing one thick finger on the unfamiliar face. "Guess who the other one is."

"Elmore," I said.

"Wrong. It's Walter Enright. Former vice president of Beltway Savings Bank, Bethesda, Maryland." Mike shuffled some faxes he held and then adjusted his bifocals. "Dixon was a clerk at the same bank," he said. " 'Bout two years ago, Enright disappeared. Kissed the wife good-bye one morning, told her he'd be home for lunch, got in his car, and vanished. They found the car at National Airport with the keys in it. A guy who was probably Enright paid cash for a set of luggage at one of the terminal shops. The same guy, apparently, also bought a ticket to Pittsburgh on USAir, still paying cash. The feds lost the trail at Pittsburgh."

"The feds," I said.

"Yeah, the fuckin' feds. It seems that when Enright vanished, half a million dollars of the bank's money went with him. There was an audit the week after he left, which was probably why he split right then. FBI thought he probably had help skimming the money, but they couldn't pin it to anyone. Then about a year later, Dixon does his own vanishing act. Left even less of a trail than Enright did. His car was

85

still in his garage, and he wasn't married. The feds were real glad to hear we'd found him, but not so glad to hear about him and Enright both being dead. The way they reacted, you'd think we killed the sons of bitches.''

"You think Dixon tracked him down," I said.

Mike shrugged. "Or else it was all arranged ahead of time, gettin' together to split the money, something like that. Except somebody got greedy, I guess. Just your basic falling out among thieves.''

I frowned. "But if Enright had decided to keep the money instead of splitting it with Dixon, why go where Dixon would be able to follow him? Why not just take off in a different direction?''

"Maybe he was planning all along to get rid of Dixon, cut the last connection to his old life. One less person lookin' for him that way.''

I nodded. "Or maybe he'd spent all the money by the time Dixon got here," I said.

Mike turned over another sheet. "Well, he'd spent a shit-pot full of it, that's for sure. His investments and bank accounts and what-all come to about four hundred grand. Most of that was for the house and the dealership.''

"So there's a hundred thousand dollars unaccounted for," I said.

"Maybe. Unless he just pissed it away without leaving much trace. Or stashed it somewhere else. Different accounts, different names.''

"Or in a suitcase behind the furnace," I said.

"Yeah, I thought of that." Mike scratched the stubble on his chin, looking doubtful. "But I can't see why he'd keep it there instead of just bankin' it like he did the rest.''

"Maybe for a quick getaway.''

"Or maybe he liked to run his fingers through it on cold nights. Who knows? The question is, where does it lead? I'm fucked if I can see. The FBI can't give us serial numbers. Enright wasn't that dumb.''

86

"A hundred grand would make a pretty good motive for murder," I said.

"Better than that stuff about him being queer, you mean? Yeah, except that the killing looks like a spur-of-the-moment deal to me, and anybody who killed him for the money—if there was any money—would have had to know it was there already. The way it was hid, you couldn't exactly trip over it while you were lookin' for the john."

"Somebody knew it was there," I said. "Somebody drew a map."

Mike nodded, fooling with his wedding ring. "Which the Skubitz girl ended up with," he said, not looking at me. "I been thinkin' about that."

I waited.

"Here's what could've happened," he said. "Tell me if you see any holes. Eddie Skubitz hangs around with Enright, and he finds out about the money some way. Also the body. He draws the map, gives it to his sister. Maybe he don't tell her what it is. Then he kills Enright, takes the money, and stashes it somewhere before he gets picked up. The sister doesn't know what the map's all about, but she figures it's important, so she goes around to have a look. That's as far as I've gotten. What do you think?"

What I thought was that if Eddie knew there was money behind the furnace and planned to steal it, he'd have had no reason to make a map, let alone give it to Marcie, unless his plan for stealing it had included her. Maybe he'd figured she'd have better opportunities than he would to get her hands on it—which could mean that it was Marcie who had killed Enright. Except that she hadn't gotten the money. Because, if she had, why come back to the house later, with the map? Maybe she'd only done part of the job—killed Enright, but then panicked and ran, without the loot. But then who had gotten it? If Eddie, why hadn't he told Marcie? He'd had plenty of chances to talk to her, even in jail. If there was money involved, there had to be someone else in the picture.

But maybe there wasn't any. Or maybe even if there was it had nothing to do with the murder.

Mike was watching me, waiting to hear what I was thinking.

"Assuming there was any money," I told him, "and assuming that that was the motive for the Enright murder . . ."

"Assuming, assuming, assuming," he broke in. I was surprised by how angry he suddenly seemed. "The more I think about that imaginary hundred grand," he said, "the less I like it. It seems to make it all simpler, but really it just fucks everything up worse than before. I say, screw the goddamn money."

"I don't think the feds'll feel that way," I said.

"Well, screw them, too," he said, then gave an embarrassed grin.

The one thing I felt sure about was that I'd been wrong about Mike, that he was still a pro and that he was on the case. It made me wonder who else I'd been wrong about, and how far.

"There's one thing the money is making us all forget about," Mike said.

I looked at him and waited.

"The body in the flower bed and the fact that someone knew that was there, too," he said. "If it was all about stealing the fuckin' money, why was the body on the map?"

It was still early when I got to Marcie's place. I had to knock a couple of times before she came to the door, looking sleepy and hostile. She had bags under her eyes and wore a ratty blue housecoat that was about three sizes too large for her, and I guessed she hadn't gotten much more sleep than I had.

"You decided to arrest me, after all," she said.

I shook my head. "Not yet," I said. "I just want to talk."

She made a sour face, but then stepped back out of the way. I opened the screen and went in. She sat primly in the rocker, arranging the big old housecoat around her legs. I sat on the sofa, feeling the heat of the day ahead already under my arms, feeling like a stranger. I began by telling her what we knew about Enright and Dixon, trying to gauge whether or not it was something she already knew about. It didn't appear to be.

"Funny," she said when I'd finished. "Everyone talking about what a noble guy he was to help Eddie out, and it turns out he was a thief and a killer. Right there on Circle Street, fitting right in with all the rest of them." She had a little twisted smile on her face, as though it all just confirmed something she'd suspected.

"The police are thinking about the missing money as a possible motive for Enright's killing," I told her. "They're going to want to find it. Right now, they're thinking that Eddie might have taken it and hid it somewhere. They'll probably be around to talk to you about that."

She gave me a funny look. "Why do you say 'they'?" she asked. "You're the police. You're the one coming around to talk to me."

That threw me for a second, but I shook my head and said, "I mean Captain Farrar. It's his investigation. I'm not here about that. I'm not convinced the money had anything to do with the murder. Or even that there was any money."

Her eyes dropped, and she tugged the bathrobe a little tighter at her throat. "You've got your own idea," she said.

I nodded, then began telling her what Eddie had said to me the night I'd talked to him, the hypothetical case he'd put to me, and how I'd had the impression he was shielding someone else.

"After I talked to you," I said, "the next day, I got the idea that maybe there'd been something going on between Enright and Eddie, that maybe Enright was a homosexual who'd somehow gotten Eddie under his thumb, and that it was himself Eddie was talking about. It would have explained why he didn't want to tell us what had happened, and it would have made the suicide make sense.''

Marcie was looking at me with round, surprised eyes, but there was an intent look on her face, too, as though it were a possibility she was thinking about for the first time.

I waited for her to say something. After a moment, she asked, ''So what did you tell Eddie?''

''I told him that it might not be self-defense, exactly, in the situation he described, because it's obvious the killer didn't stop hitting Enright until he was dead. But it's not first-degree murder, either, not premeditated. Maybe no more than involuntary manslaughter, something like that.'' I hesitated, then said, ''A young person in that situation, being mistreated by an older man, finally striking back . . . if that person confessed, and had a good attorney, they probably wouldn't have to do much time. Maybe none at all.''

Marcie gave me a bemused smile. ''You think I did it,'' she said. ''That's what you've been putting together in your head. Why you came out here to see me.''

''I'm not sure,'' I said. ''If I were sure . . .'' I was going to say I'd arrest her, but then I realized I wasn't even sure about that. I shook my head. ''Do you know of anybody else Eddie would have been willing to go to prison to protect?''

She frowned but didn't answer.

''I'm just here to tell you what I told Eddie,'' I said. ''If you did do it, or if you know anything about it, the best thing is to come clean.'' I paused, listening to myself, to how I sounded. ''That's not it,'' I said. ''Really, it's just that I'd like to know how big a fool I've been, what it is I've been missing. That's what I came out here to find out.''

Her look softened, but then she said, ''That's not something you're going to find out here, Johnny. Anyway, you don't really trust me now. You wouldn't believe anything I told you.'' Her gaze turned inward. ''That means I can't trust you,'' she said. ''I just have to work this out on my own.''

''Tell me what you can,'' I said. ''We can work together.''

She stared at me for a moment, then said, "Eddie was the only person in the world who I knew for sure was always on my side, no matter what. Can you tell me you're on my side that way?"

She waited while I thought about it. I thought about what I would have said if Terry Gardens had asked me that same question before everything had gone bad. "I've got to know," I said. "I can't tell what side I'm on without knowing what's going on."

"You've chosen your side," she said. "You're a cop. You're on Bullard's side, and Dexter's side. And believe me, you don't know what's going on there, either. But you're going to have to find it out for yourself. We're on our own now, Johnny. Each of us. That's just the way it is." She didn't seem very happy about it, but she seemed resigned to it, beyond persuasion.

We both sat silently for a long time, looking at each other, as though we were both trying to think of something to say that might bridge the gap between us, and failing, and after a while I got up and left.

CHAPTER
NINE

When I checked in on the two-way, the dispatcher told me that Bullard wanted to see me. When I got to his office, he was sitting behind his big desk with his bad arm lying in front of him, staring at it. He looked like he was concentrating hard, and it occurred to me that he was trying to flex the fingers—that it was something I'd seen him do before without realizing it. I stood and waited until he gave up and looked at me.

"Sit down," he said. "Tell me about the girl."

I hesitated for a second, then began telling him about the break-in at the Enright place.

"Not that," he said. "I've read the report."

"What then?"

"You interrogated her last night, but you didn't file any report on that. Then you let her go, and then you went out to see her first thing this morning. And as far as I know you haven't talked to Mike about any of this. I want to know what's going on."

I nodded and began telling him about the compact and what I thought it might mean, about Marcie maybe having an affair with Enright, and how it seemed to me to tie in with what Eddie had told me the night before he killed himself.

When I paused, collecting my thoughts about the conversation I'd just had with Marcie, Bullard said, "Go back to this business about the compact. Did she tell you she got it from Enright?"

"Not in so many words. She didn't deny it."

"Do you have any other reason to believe she was seeing Enright?"

I thought about that. "No," I said. "It just makes sense to me." Saying that made me feel cold inside, but it was true.

Bullard gave me a funny look. "It does, huh?" he said. "Well, it doesn't make a hell of a lot of sense to me. I can believe Enright might have had something going with a truck-stop waitress, and even that he might have wanted to keep it a secret, so he wouldn't look like a fool. What I can't believe is that he would have managed to keep it a secret in Elk Rapids. Someone would have known, or guessed. People on Circle Street, the other girls at the truck stop. Someone. There would have been talk. And there hasn't been any at all, that I know of. Nobody keeps a secret that well in Elk Rapids, especially not an outsider."

"He did a pretty good job of keeping secret who he really was."

Bullard shrugged. "That's different. That all happened somewhere else. Look, instead of trying to imagine some secret affair, isn't it more reasonable to suppose that Eddie knew about the hundred grand, that he killed Enright for it, and that he gave Marcie the compact with the map and key in it? I mean, doesn't that really make more sense?"

I shrugged. "We don't know the money existed, either," I pointed out. "But if you take that line, then you have the problem that neither of the Skubitz kids ended up with the money. If they had, there'd be no reason for Marcie to go back to the house with the map. And why make a map in the first place? If Eddie . . ."

Bullard waved his good hand at me impatiently, and I shut up.

"You're talking about them like they're a couple of pros," he said. "These are just two small-town kids who saw a chance to grab a bunch of money, and it all went bad somehow. My guess is they never meant to kill Enright, but something went wrong. Who knows why they did this or that, why they made a map, whatever? They probably didn't know. There are always questions like that that don't get answered. The only important question is who did it, and unless you've got a better suspect we don't know about, it looks to me like one or both of the Skubitz kids."

I shrugged. It ended up the same place, either way. "So you're going to arrest Marcie?" I asked.

"Not just yet. We haven't got a case against her for anything except B and E. What I'm interested in is finding the money."

"If there is any."

Bullard studied me for a moment. "I'm convinced there is," he said. "And I'm pretty sure Marcie Skubitz knows where it is. Maybe she doesn't know she knows."

I didn't say anything.

"You don't agree," Bullard said.

I shook my head. "I don't really think the money has anything to do with it," I said. "But it's not my case."

"That's the point I'm trying to get to," Bullard said. "You've been going around acting like it still is."

"Mike said it was okay. . . ."

"He said for you to keep him informed, didn't he?"

I nodded. It was obvious Bullard and Mike had been talking about me, and I found that I didn't like it.

"From where I sit," Bullard said, "you've been playing it pretty close to the vest. You haven't let Mike in on any of this."

"Did he complain?"

Bullard shook his head. "I'm the one that's complaining," he said. "You seem to be playing your own game here, and I'm not sure what it is."

I blinked at him. I wasn't sure, either, but I couldn't tell him that.

"If it's just that you like the girl," Bullard said, "I could understand that. But you've still got to remember you're a cop."

He was saying the same thing Marcie had, I realized. Which side was I on? All I could say to him was the same thing I'd said to her.

"I've got to know what's going on," I told him.

He gave me a long, impassive stare. "I hope you don't mean . . ." he began.

"All I mean," I said, "is that I don't know what's going on. Things aren't as simple as everyone seems to want to think they are. Eddie was the easy suspect and we grabbed him, because of the two hundred dollars, but it turned out he was telling the truth about that. Now there's this other money that we don't even know exists, and everyone wants to act like that solves everything."

"You don't mean everyone," Bullard said quietly. "You mean me."

I didn't say anything.

"I'll tell you how it looks from where I sit," Bullard said. "I've got a case with some unanswered questions, but it's not much different from a lot of other cases, really. Someone killed someone else and there's apparently some money missing. There were only one or two people who had any known motive or opportunity, and experience tells me they're the ones who did it. All we have to do is nail down the details, answer as many of the questions as we can. That's what it always comes down to. But in the middle of this, I've got a detective who's still trying to square things for something that happened two years ago. And now he's gotten himself in a bind again, involved with another girl who's in the middle of something, and he's afraid of it all coming apart again and falling in on him, the way it did before, and so he's running around in a panic, getting in everyone else's way, screwing things up." He stopped talking and waited for me to say something, watching me with a challenging expression, but also with something like compassion. It reminded me of the way Dexter had looked at me, up in his office, and suddenly made me feel sick with buried anger. I wasn't even sure who I was angry at, because I couldn't say Bullard was wrong.

"All I can say," I said stubbornly, "is that I need to know what's going on."

Bullard nodded impatiently. "For the time being," he said, "just for the time being, I want your badge and gun." He tapped his desk top with the fingers of his good hand.

I felt something wash over my body, the nerve-endings growing numb, the way you feel when you dive into cold water. There was a cold fist clenched in my belly. "You mean I'm suspended?" I said.

"Let's call it a vacation. I don't think you'll be able to keep away from this case, even if I order you to, so I'm going to take you out of action for a while, until Mike's got it wrapped up. After that, we'll talk. I think you need to do some serious thinking about what you want to do. I don't mean just Elk Rapids. I mean whether you really want to be a cop anymore. Maybe you'll never be able to handle what happened in Kansas City. It's hard for a cop to see somebody walk away from something like that, even if the somebody is you. You can't ever pay back for that, and that may be something you can't live with—not and stay a cop. You think about it."

There was a silence, and after a while I stood up and fumbled for my wallet with thick fingers. Bullard watched me dig out the badge and drop it on his desk. His eyes were sad, distant. I saw that this was the crossroad I'd been fearing, and it wasn't anything I'd expected. I still didn't know which way to go. With Bullard still watching, I unsnapped the holster from my shoulder rig and dropped it on the desk beside the badge.

Bullard didn't look at them. "Go home," he said softly.

"Do some thinking. These will be here for you when all this is over. We'll talk then."

On my way through the lobby, I passed Willis Seba, and he did a double take at my face.

"You okay, Lieutenant?" he asked.

"I'm fine," I said, more loudly than I'd intended. "Nothing I can't handle." I stopped for a moment at the double glass doors, looking at the sidewalk outside, and said it again, hoping it would sound more convincing to me: "Nothing I can't handle."

I handled it by getting drunk for the first time in two years. The last time had been the night after the Internal Affairs guys took my badge and gun in Kansas City. I wondered if maybe there was a pattern there.

I started off with beer at the Happy Jack Tavern, a working-man's dive, about as far from the Blue Tattoo as you could get. By the time I got back to my apartment overlooking the old railway depot, I'd picked up a fifth of scotch somewhere along the way. I made myself a scotch on the rocks and sat down in the armchair in front of the little black-and-white TV, hoping there might be a baseball game on, but there wasn't. So I watched what there was, which was mostly people walking around the furniture in a living room, talking, saying things to each other that I couldn't follow. Every now and then one of them would say something a little louder than before, and then pause, and a bunch of other people somewhere off camera would laugh uproariously for no apparent reason. At some point, it got to be too much trouble to get up for ice, so I let that go, and then later on it got to be almost impossible to pour the stuff into the glass, so I dropped that off the arm of the chair and nursed the bottle. I guess I must have had the idea of taking a shower, somewhere in there, because I woke up on my sofa, stark naked, the empty bottle clutched to my chest.

The TV was still on, making a high-pitched sound, but

that wasn't what had awakened me. It was the pounding on the door.

"Who is it?" I said, but it came out as "umm mum mum."

"Johnny?" It was a female voice, far away.

Marcie, I thought, come to tell me everything. To confess, or to tell me it had all been a mistake. No affair, no murder.

"A minute," I managed, not very loudly. I let the bottle go and rolled over on my side, trying to push myself up with my arms, but I didn't have much success. I heard the door open. A light came on somewhere, making me close my eyes. Someone knelt beside me and put a cool hand on my forehead.

"Jesus, Johnny," she said.

I squinted at her. It wasn't Marcie. Her face was blurry, but I thought I knew who it was. "Terry," I said. "Terry." I reached for her and tried to pulled her down to me, but she pulled loose easily.

"Pretty ambitious for a guy who can't even make it to the bathroom," she said.

I remembered that I was naked, but I couldn't remember where my clothes were. It was like one of those dreams where you're out in public naked, except I knew I wasn't dreaming. For some reason, it struck me as funny, and I started giggling.

"Johnny," she said, "I need your help."

That was even funnier. I giggled some more. She slapped me, hard. I could barely feel it, but it still made me mad. I tried to get up, but I wound up stretched out on the floor beside the couch, the liquor bottle under my ribs. I started crying, and then I felt sick, and then after a while I went back to sleep.

CHAPTER
TEN

I woke up in bed with a couple of pillows stacked up behind me, and Clarice Lucas sitting on a chair beside the bed.

"You ready to drink some coffee?" she asked.

I nodded. "And aspirin," I said.

"Where do you keep it?"

I shook my head.

She got up. "I'll see what I have in my purse." She came back in a few minutes with three Darvons and a glass of water. I sat up to take it. Sitting up made my head pound.

"Jesus," I said. "You don't have any of those pills your brother takes, do you?"

She smiled and shook her head. "I don't use them," she said. She left again and came back a few minutes later with a cup of coffee and a saucer.

I took it and sipped. I felt lousy, but I seemed to be back in control of my body, more or less.

"You got me in here and put me to bed all by yourself?" I asked.

"I've had a lot of experience," she said. "Speaking of which . . ."

"Rob," I said.

She nodded. There were suddenly tears in her eyes, or maybe they'd been there all along and I hadn't noticed. "I told you the other night that I was waiting up for him," she said. "But he never came back. I don't know where he is." She wiped a hand across her face and gave a little sniff.

"The police . . ." I said.

"I wanted to ask you personally. You helped after the accident. There's no telling where they might find him. In what circumstances."

"I'm not on the force right now," I said. "I'm . . . on vacation." I gave a harsh laugh that hurt both my throat and my head.

Clarice cocked her head to one side and studied me for a moment, then said, "Well, all the better. I can hire you privately to look for him."

Hey, my first case, I thought. Today is the first day of the rest of my life. It didn't cheer me up. Anyway, I didn't have a PI license.

"What time is it?" I asked.

"About seven."

"A.M.?"

"Yes. It's Sunday morning."

"You stayed up all night with me?"

She shook her head. "I slept some. I'm fine."

I started to get out of bed, then had to slow down as the chimes rang again in my head. I noticed I was wearing a clean pair of boxer shorts. She'd probably washed me off, too.

"If the politics or the psychology doesn't work out," I said, "you could get a job as a practical nurse."

"Nice to know," she said. "I'll wait in the living room while you get dressed."

"What probably happened," I told her later, when we were sitting at the kitchen table, sipping more coffee, "is that he made the rounds of the bars and picked up someone or got picked up at some point, and now he's shacked up somewhere."

"For two days?"

"It happens."

"I called around to all the bars."

"Did you ask if he was there, or did you ask if they'd seen him?"

"Both."

"Well, somebody's seen him," I said. "You can count on that. They might not tell you, over the phone. They might think you were his wife and they were doing him a favor."

"So what do we do?"

I got up, still a little shaky, and put on my jacket. The shoulder rig, minus the holster, was hanging on one of the knobs of my chest of drawers. I felt funny leaving it there. "I have a couple of ideas," I said. "You sit tight. I'll be back in less than an hour."

If Rob was lying up somewhere along the bar circuit, I figured Dexter Gennaro might be able to find out where, especially if he and Rob were as tight as Rob had suggested the night I'd met him. The truck stop was as busy as always, but the parking lot in front of the Blue Tattoo was empty except for a single car parked near the front door—a beat-up Toyota station wagon with a caduceus on the front windshield. Maybe if you were as important as Dexter, you could even get doctors to make house calls.

The front door was unlocked. Halfway up the stairs, I heard the murmur of men's voices. I went up more slowly, expecting Nick to appear at any moment, but he didn't. The door to Dexter's office was standing partway open, and I could make out the voices clearly now—Dexter's and another man's, someone I recognized vaguely but couldn't place. I stood still for a moment, listening.

"It's really your problem," Dexter was saying.

"If everything comes out, it's your problem, too," the other man said.

"Not if you don't say anything."

"Not say anything? You think, if I'm going to prison I won't . . ."

"Easy, doc. No one's talking about prison yet. Anyway, there are worse things than prison."

There was a little silence and then the second man, his voice quavering slightly, said, "I'm not sure that's true, for someone like me."

"Believe me," Dexter said, "it's true. You want to try to relax, doctor, not get to feeling desperate. Desperate men make other people nervous."

I'd placed the other voice by now. It was Dr. Blaine, one of the local physicians who sometimes helped out the coroner by serving as medical examiner.

"All right," he was saying. "I'll be all right. I understand what you're saying."

"Good. I'm glad to hear it."

"But you have to understand . . . things are getting beyond my control. And now these murders . . ."

"Have nothing to do with us," Dexter said. "Unless you know something I don't know."

"No, no. It's just . . . it gets the police involved."

"Not with us. Believe me, Chief Bullard is a good friend of mine and I can assure you that the police have absolutely no interest in you and me."

"But Rob . . . he found the body, and then there was that wreck. And they kept his pills. . . ." His voice rose slightly on the last word, as though he were becoming hysterical.

"So what? They're legal, aren't they?"

"Yes, but . . . you can't count too heavily on those prescriptions, Dexter. If an examining board were to look into it . . ."

"Why should they? Rob's not going to say anything. He doesn't know anything to say."

"But he's out of control. He's an addict. It's reached the point where I've got to give him all the pills he wants or give him none at all. There's no middle ground. And either way, he's a danger to himself . . . to us. He needs treatment."

"Soon, doctor. Soon. I'm as concerned about Rob as you

are, believe me. Nick will find him and bring him home and tuck him into bed. And then it's just a few weeks to the primary and then two months to the general election, and after that we'll figure a way to get Rob the treatment he needs. Less than four months. Just keep him on his feet that long.''

''I don't know if I can. . . .''

''You have to.'' Something changed in Dexter's voice. ''Keep in mind the other business we've done.''

There was a short silence. Then the doctor said, ''You wouldn't . . . that would hurt you as much as me. . . .''

''Would it? I'm not sure. No money changed hands. A prosecutor might see me as just a misguided intermediary between the drug doctor and his rich clients, someone you were using to keep yourself insulated, especially if I were willing to cooperate. You see, doctor, there's always more than one way of looking at things. It's all in the perspective.''

''I'm no drug dealer,'' Blaine said in a hoarse voice.

''Not from your perspective. Maybe not even from mine. But what about a jury's, doctor? That's what would matter, after all.''

There was a long silence. Then Blaine said, ''All right. Just find him. I've got to get back. Eloise will be getting home from church.''

I stepped quickly past the stairway into the darkness at the other end of the hallway and watched from there as Blaine came out and went down the stairs, his shoulders hunched. I waited until I'd heard the door open and close, then went quietly back down the stairs, watched through the window as he drove off, then opened the door and closed it again, and went back up the stairs, making as much noise as I could.

Dexter came out of his office and met me at the top with a slightly troubled smile.

''You working today?'' I asked him. ''It's a Sunday.''

''No rest for the wicked,'' he said. ''What about yourself?''

"I'm off duty at the moment. Just doing a favor for Clarice Lucas. Her brother didn't come home the last two nights and I'm trying to track him down."

Dexter nodded. "I know," he said. "She called here last night. I've got Nick Adrian out looking for him. Come on in the office."

We went in and sat down.

"Had he been here?" I asked.

Dexter shook his head. "And that's unusual," he said. "Normally, he'll start out here. But he wasn't here Friday night at all—or last night, for that matter." He pursed his lips, looking genuinely concerned.

"That's pretty generous of you, to have one of your employees look for him on a Sunday," I said. "Probably have to pay him overtime. Rob must be a close friend."

Dexter smiled and shrugged. "I knew his father," he said. "I guess I feel sort of responsible for him now. Clarice, too. Like an old uncle, you know?" He laughed. "Of course, Rob's a grown man. But we don't want him getting in trouble. He's probably going to be the next state representative from this district, after all."

"Just good business," I said.

"There's that way of looking at it," Dexter agreed pleasantly. "Besides, it gives Nick something to do. Life around here is a little dull, compared to what he's used to."

"Really? What's he used to?" I asked.

"Oh . . . well, you know . . . I only meant, living back east, in the big city. Life's just slower here, that's all. Slower than Kansas City, too, I'd guess."

I nodded and stood up. "It has its moments here," I said. "Listen, I promised Miss Lucas I'd take care of this, you understand?" I waited for him to give a little nod, then said, "So when Nick finds him, let me know. I want to be involved."

Dexter gave me a calculating look, but nodded. "I'll do that," he said. "You be at the station?"

I shook my head. "At home. I'm kind of on vacation right now."

He nodded again, obviously curious about that, but not wanting to ask. "Well," he said, "have a good time."

Clarice had been straightening up the apartment.

"You didn't strike me as the domestic type," I said.

"It's the early training," she said. "You never quite shake it. What about Rob?"

"Not yet," I said, "but soon, I think. Right now we wait."

"For what?"

"Dexter Gennaro. He's looking, and he's probably got better connections for this than I do."

She looked thoughtful for a moment, and then nodded. "Yes," she said. "That's a good idea."

"You know him?"

She hesitated, then said, "Oh, not really. He was a friend of my father. And now of Rob, I guess."

It didn't sound as though she thought of Dexter as her old uncle. I wondered how much she understood about Rob's drug problem, but I decided to wait until her brother was found before saying anything about it. She was obviously worried enough already.

I went into the kitchen and found a pint of scotch I'd bought a long time ago, for a poker game with Mike and some of the other guys. Hair of the dog. I poured out half a glass, took a sip, then changed my mind and poured the rest down the sink. I went to the icebox and got a beer instead. But when I'd popped the top, I found I didn't want that very badly either. I carried it back to the living room, hoping the mood would pass.

"I'm sorry to get you involved in all this during your vacation," she said.

I laughed. "I'm not on vacation," I said. "I've been suspended."

"Suspended? Why?"

I thought about it. "Insubordination, I guess. Chief Bullard and I had a disagreement."

"So you're not investigating the murders?"

"I never was, officially. It's Mike Farrar's case."

"But you were there both times. At the Elmore house."

"Enright," I said. "His name was Walter Enright."

"Yes. I read it in the paper this morning. But I can't get used to thinking of him by a different name. And there's supposed to be some money missing, isn't there?"

"Maybe a hundred grand. That's how much is still unaccounted for."

"Goodness. To think about him living right there among us all the time, with a body in the garden." She gave a quizzical smile. "How did you know where to look for the body?" she asked.

"We had a map."

"A map? Where'd you get it?"

"The Skubitz girl had it. We took it from her the night she broke in over there."

"Oh." She thought about it for a moment. "So she must have been involved," she said. "She and her brother. They must have killed him for the money."

"That's what the chief thinks," I said.

Clarice's eyes widened. "You don't agree?"

I shrugged. I didn't want to get into it all again. I was feeling glad that Clarice had brought me this new problem to think about. "I don't agree about the money," I said. "We don't even know it exists, really."

"That doesn't seem like much of a disagreement," she said. "I mean, to get suspended for."

"There's more to it than that," I said. "It's between Bullard and me. Going back to Kansas City."

"You don't have to tell me about it," she said, obviously intending it as an invitation to do so.

I smiled at her. "Maybe I'll get an appointment with you, after you're in practice," I said. Once I'd said it, I realized it might not be a bad idea—maybe not Clarice, but someone, a professional.

Clarice nodded. "I was so sorry to hear about that boy killing himself," she said.

I looked at her. She seemed to mean it. "Even if he bashed Enright's head in?" I asked.

"Who knows what the circumstances may have been? Obviously, Enright wasn't really a very nice man. And Eddie always seemed like a sweet, timid boy. Always eager to please. I always thought he had a crush on me."

"Eddie?"

"Yes." She gave a sad little laugh. "I'd see him over at Elmore's . . . Enright's . . . sometimes, when we were visiting, or I'd go jogging and he'd be out in the yard, doing some chores. And he'd always stop to talk. . . ." She laughed again. "Well, he didn't exactly talk. He was too shy. He'd stand around trying to think of something to say, hoping I'd say something to him." She shook her head. There was a small tear in the corner of one eye. She blinked rapidly, making it disappear.

"What did you think of Enright?" I asked.

She shrugged, her expression losing some of its softness. "He was very quiet and mostly kept to himself," she said. "I would have said he seemed like a nice enough man. Everyone liked what he was doing for Eddie, although there were some who thought he was being foolish."

"Lowell Harrison?"

She laughed. "Mainly him," she said. Her smile faded. "I was surprised to hear about that . . . about Enright and the girl. Eddie's sister." She gave me a sidelong look that told me she'd also heard about me and Eddie's sister.

"Was that in the paper, too?" I asked.

"No. But it's a small town. News like that travels fast."

"I suppose it does." I thought about Marcie working at the truck stop, the diners whispering behind their menus.

The telephone rang.

"This is Dexter," the voice at the other end said. "Nick found him."

"Where?"

"At a whorehouse in Independence. Place called Burns House on Oak Street. Supposed to be an apartment building."

"Trouble?" I asked.

"Could be. Some of those places are connected, mostly out of Oklahoma City, but Kansas City has been moving in the last couple of years. So there's tension."

I was interested in Dexter knowing about something like that, but I decided to ask him about it later. "Where's Adrian now?" I asked.

"Waiting for you, at a little corner shopping center a block from the place. He's driving a black Lamborghini."

"Whoa," I said. "You must pay well."

He laughed. We both knew his local reputation as a skinflint. "He had it when he came," he said. "What I pay him probably doesn't cover the insurance."

"Where is he?" Clarice asked when I'd hung up.

I hesitated, then decided there was little point in equivocating. "At a whorehouse in Independence," I said. "One of Dexter's employees is keeping an eye on the place until I get there." I went to the bedroom and got out the .357 magnum I'd bought when I was younger and thought there was something manly about a big, powerful gun. I checked the load, clipped the holster to my shoulder rig, shrugged it on, and went back to the living room for my jacket.

Clarice's eyes widened. "Why do you think you'll need that?" she asked.

"I don't know that I will," I said. "But places like that can be mob-connected. It's just possible someone lured him there, figuring to make something out of it. If so, I hope to persuade them to think differently."

She nodded. "I'm going with you," she said.

"I don't think so."

"I'm not going to argue about it. He's my brother."

I thought about it and then shrugged. "Okay," I said. "Just don't flash that designer gun unless I tell you to."

CHAPTER
ELEVEN

Nick Adrian was just as perfect as he'd been the first time I'd met him, although instead of a suit he was wearing slacks and an open-necked shirt with a small gold chain. He looked like he'd just come from the barber, or maybe the hairdresser. I wondered if these were his leisure clothes or his work clothes.

He was lounging against the fender of his sleek, black car. He gave me an accusing smile as I got out and walked toward him. "You brought a date," he said.

"It's Lucas's sister," I said.

He leaned over slightly, looked past me, and gave a friendly little wave, just the nice young man from down the street, probably on his way to the golf course.

"That's your wheels, huh?" he said, giving the Celica the once-over. "We'd better take mine, case we have to make a quick getaway."

"Don't judge a book by its cover," I said.

"Oh, I'm sure your car does just fine, whenever you can get it started."

I shrugged and went back to Clarice. "We'll go in his car," I said.

She nodded and got out. As we walked back toward Adrian, she headed toward the passenger side, but he intercepted her, putting a hand on her arm. "You're the driver on this job," he said.

She looked at me. I nodded. Seeing the two of them standing together that way—two tall, stylish people posed in front of a black Lamborghini—made me feel suddenly rumpled and ordinary, a fifth wheel. I shook my head in self-disgust and squeezed into the backseat. Clarice slid into the driver's seat and adjusted the seat and the mirror as though she'd been driving Lamborghinis all her life. Adrian got into the passenger side.

"It's a block down, on the right," Adrian told her.

"We passed it coming in," Clarice said. "Shall I go there now?"

"You know what kind of place it is?"

"Yes." Clarice started the car and put it in gear with the clutch down, letting it idle.

"I like her," Adrian said to me. "Maybe it's her who should be running for the legislature."

"You haven't seen my brother at his best," Clarice said, looking straight ahead.

"I hope to God that's true. Okay," he said. "Let's go past it slowly. I'm going to have you let us out at the corner." Once we were moving, he looked back at me and said, "You carrying?"

I pulled back the edge of the jacket and showed him the magnum.

"That'll come in handy if we run into a wounded elephant," he said. "Until then, how about we see how far we can get with this and a kind word?" He opened his palm and showed me a black switchblade with inlaid silver trim. Clarice glanced once at it and looked away again expressionlessly.

"You and Clarice must shop at the same armory," I said.

"It's what's inside that counts. Stop here."

Clarice slowed and pulled to the curb in front of a darkened drugstore.

"It looks just like a regular neighborhood," she said.

"It is," Adrian said. "There's a similar establishment on the other side of the street—that brick building with the awnings—but the rest are just ordinary apartment houses. Nice and quiet and discreet. You could sit here a long time before you figured out what was going on."

"You sure he's still inside?" I asked.

"Positive."

"You got a plan?"

He shrugged. "I figured we'd just walk inside like a couple of horny yuppies, and play it by ear."

"I don't look the part," I said.

"That's true. We'll pretend you're a homeless person I'm treating."

"While you guys are working up your comedy act, my brother's still inside there," Clarice said.

Adrian grinned at her. "Okay," he said. He looked back at me. "You got your shield, case we need to bluff?"

I shook my head.

He was silent a moment, perhaps waiting for me to explain, then shrugged. "Elk Rapids badge probably wouldn't impress anyone around here anyway," he said. He put a hand on Clarice's shoulder. She flinched slightly and her chin came up. I felt a tug in my gut that felt oddly like jealousy.

"Relax," Adrian said to her. "Everything's going to be fine. After we get out, I want you to drive around the block to the other end of the alley that runs beside the building. You know where that is?"

She nodded.

"I figure about twenty minutes," he said. "Watch for us to come out the side door. When you see us, hit the gas. We may need to make a quick exit. If . . . oh, let's say forty-five minutes goes by and you haven't seen us yet, drive back here and park in front of the drugstore again, and use that pay phone over there to call Dexter at the Blue Tattoo."

"Not the police?"

"Not unless you want all this on the evening news."

"Okay," she said.

Adrian and I got out and walked back along the sidewalk toward the Burns House. The name was carved in stone above the front door. Other than that, the only lettering on the building was a small sign in one of the front windows saying "Rooms—Reasonable Rates." Inside the outer doors was a tiny foyer and a second, locked door with a single button beside it. Adrian pushed it.

There was a bing-bong sound somewhere far inside. We waited, assuming an air of nervous, but innocent, expectancy. Or at least I did. Adrian looked more like someone getting ready to yell trick or treat.

The door was opened by a tiny black woman wearing a black and white French maid's outfit and a deeply dimpled smile. "Come on in," she said. "You lookin' for a room?" She gave Adrian a careful second look, her eyes narrowing slightly.

"Not for more than an hour," he said, smiling back politely. She nodded, gave me a second glance, then turned and led us into the parlor, which was cheerfully and sedately furnished—overstuffed chairs, pictures of birds and dogs on the walls, a silver tray on the coffee table with glasses on it, and a small bar against one wall.

"Fix yourself a drink," she said. "Make yourselves at home. I'll go see if any of the rooms are free right now."

"We'd like to talk to the housemother first," Adrian said.

The black girl paused. "You mean the manager, Mrs. Jackson? She's not here. She's in church." It sounded like she meant it.

"Then you'll do," Adrian said.

She dropped the little-girl niceness. "You aren't really customers," she said. "What the hell you want?"

"A guy came in night before last," I said. "Big guy, handsome, well-dressed. He's still here. We've come to take him home."

"Wouldn't want him to overstay his welcome," Adrian said pleasantly.

She looked at him and then at me, and then shook her head slightly. "You could be a cop," she said to me, "but not him. Whatever you are, you chumps are in way over your heads. Better beat it while you still can."

"Okay," Adrian said, smiling cheerfully, "we can do it the hard way."

She started to turn, but she wasn't quick enough. Adrian spun her around, encircled both arms and her waist with his left arm, and held the switchblade in front of her face. As she stared at it, the blade flicked out, an inch from her nose.

"Going to behave?" he asked.

She nodded, her mouth partly open.

"Good. Where's Rob Lucas?"

"There's a guy in Debby's room. Don't know his name."

"Show us."

She seemed to get her breath and courage back all at once. "You pretty tough with the girls, ain't you?" she said. "We got some boys here, too. They'll shove that pigsticker up your white ass. You'll probably enjoy it, too."

Adrian's smile froze. He brought the blade close to her face and touched the point to her cheek, an inch or so below her eye. A tiny drop of blood appeared against the chocolate skin.

"You motherfucking faggot," she said, her voice rasping. "I'll . . ."

He let her go, took a neat step backward, like a dancer, switched the knife from his right hand to his left, and clipped her on the chin with a short, efficient punch. She went down like an empty sack.

"Too noisy," he said. "A potty mouth, too."

"Hope you know where Debby's room is," I said.

"We'll find it." He opened a nearby door, which revealed wooden steps leading down into darkness. He lifted the black girl effortlessly and rolled her through the door, closing it. I heard her thump a couple of times, as she rolled partway down the steps.

He smoothed his hair with one hand and tucked his shirt in all around. "Let's try upstairs," he said.

A narrow hallway led to an equally narrow staircase. At the top was a long hall with half a dozen closed doors with little metal numbers tacked to them, and another stairway leading further up. As we hesitated, a blond girl wearing a superfluous see-through nightgown came out of one of the doors and blinked at us uncertainly.

"Debby?" Adrian asked.

"Uhh . . . no. I'm Megan. Debby's up on three."

"Where on three?"

"Uhh . . . on the left. Second door down. But . . ."

We turned up the stairs.

". . . I think she has a guest already," Megan said behind us.

On the third floor we could hear a radio or stereo playing softly somewhere. John Denver, it sounded like, though I didn't recognize the melody. Adrian knocked on Debby's door.

"Busy," a female voice said.

We went in. The walls were papered in fuzzy red and black stripes, and there was a big mirror on the ceiling. Reflected in the mirror was Rob Lucas, sprawling naked and unconscious across the king-size bed that was the main article of furniture in the room. The only other article of furniture was an armchair opposite the door, where a dark-haired girl, dressed just like Rob except for white anklets with little blue balls on the backs, was reading a copy of *Architectural Digest*. She looked at us over the top of it, apparently not much disturbed by our entry.

"I said I was busy," she said.

"Don't let us interrupt you," Adrian said. "It's him we want." He went over to the bed and gave Rob's shoulder a shake. "Come on, big guy. Time to go home."

Rob didn't respond. For a second I thought he might be dead, but then I saw his chest move slowly in and out.

"We're gonna have to carry him," I said.

"Jesus," Adrian said. "How much did he have to drink?"

"It ain't booze," Debby said. "He's just worn out, I guess. I separate the men from the boys, honey."

"It ain't sex, either," I said. "It's some kind of drug he takes. Where's his clothes?"

"I don't think Mrs. Jackson . . ." Debby began.

Adrian grabbed his crotch. "This for Mrs. Jackson," he said. "Where's his clothes?"

"In the closet. Where else?"

Adrian opened it and began pulling them out. He checked the wallet, found it full of cash, and put it back.

"What do you think?" Debby said. "This ain't that kind of place."

"They're all that kind of place," I said.

She made a show of pretending to read her magazine again, sulking. Adrian wrestled Rob into his Jockey shorts and started pulling his trousers on.

"You want to give me a hand?" he said. "This must be what it's like to work in a mortuary."

Debby looked up. "What about my two hundred?" she asked. "I ain't been paid yet."

"You actually do anything for the two hundred, besides make redecorating plans?" Adrian asked, nodding at the magazine.

"I tried. Ain't my fault if he can't, is it? Anyway, he spent the night here. That's what the money's for."

"Right," I said. "Have the front desk send him a bill."

We got his shirt on and buttoned up, but didn't bother trying to tuck it in. I went to the closet for his jacket, and that's when I noticed the spy hole just below the heating vent.

"Shit," I said. "Where do they keep the tapes?"

"What tapes?" Debby asked.

Adrian looked around at me. I nodded at the closet and he

looked that way and then pursed his lips. "Better be quick," he said.

"The video tapes, films, photos, whatever it is they shoot through the closet," I said to Debby. "Where is it?"

"Mrs. Jackson . . ." she began.

I opened my jacket slightly to show her the .357. "I can tell that's not going to be the right answer," I said.

She looked at the gun and licked her lips. "Mrs. Jackson's *office*," she said. "In the basement."

"You take him out," I said to Adrian. "I'll check the basement."

"Don't take too long," he said. To Debby he said, "Put on a robe or something. You're going to help me get him down to the side door."

She stood up languidly, revealing the flimsy garment she'd been sitting on. "This is all I got," she said.

"Hardly worth the trouble," Adrian said, then nodding at me. "Watch out for Fifi, going down those steps."

"Who's Fifi?" Debby asked. I didn't wait to hear Adrian's answer.

I encountered no one going back down to the parlor. The basement was dark, but there was enough ambient light to see that the black girl wasn't there. I went down the steps cautiously, my hand on the gun butt. Most of the basement was unfinished concrete, but there was a fake-wood wall across one end, with two doors in it. One was locked. The other opened onto a storage room with cleaning supplies along one wall and a couple of old green file cabinets along the other. I opened one of the drawers and saw stacked videotape cassettes, each one labeled neatly with a date. I looked quickly through all the drawers, finding more tapes in each, but none with a recent date.

The other door didn't look very solid. I got a good grip on the knob, braced myself, and gave a sharp push. Fake wood splintered and gave with a sound like cardboard ripping. Inside was a regular office with a Persian rug covering most of the concrete floor. There were more file cabinets, but I checked the big lower drawer of the desk first and found what I was after: a hand-held camcorder with a tape still in it, and a couple of unmarked cassettes beside it. It took me a couple of minutes to figure out how the thing worked, but then I was able to play back enough of the tape, through the viewfinder, to tell that it was the Rob and Debby show. Not that it looked very exciting. I removed the cassette and pocketed it, then took the other two, just to be safe.

Outside the office, it seemed darker in the basement than it had before. I was at the bottom of the stairs before I realized that that was because someone had closed the door at the top. The someone was standing just inside the closed door, pointing a gun at me. He flicked on the light. He was a tall, thin man with a narrow, bloodless face. Beside him was a sweet little roly-poly woman of about fifty with silver-white hair.

"Church out already?" I asked.

"See if he's got a gun," the woman said. Her voice didn't sound sweet.

The man started carefully down the stairs, keeping his own gun pointed unwaveringly at my midsection. He was halfway down when the door at the top opened and Nick Adrian stepped through and put his knife against Mrs. Jackson's throat.

"Toss the gun," Adrian said. "I want to hear it hit the far wall."

The man hesitated, the gun and his gaze wavering back and forth between me and Adrian. In the instant of silence, Mrs. Jackson put an elbow into Adrian's stomach, ducked under the blade, and vaulted the railing like a gymnast. Maybe she'd been one once; if so, she lost points on the landing, coming down on the side of one ankle and giving a shriek of pain, winding up on her hands and knees. Adrian looked at her with surprise, then looked back at the gun pointed at him.

I don't know how he planned to handle that. I didn't wait to find out. I put two bullets into the big man's back, the .357 going off like a bomb in the small space, making my ears ring. The man went down, his gun slipping from his hand. Mrs. Jackson made a game move for it, bad ankle and all, but I kicked it away and then gave her a kick on the side of the head to keep her quiet for a while. She flopped over on her back and didn't move.

"Let's haul ass," Adrian said.

The black girl was on the phone in the parlor. When she saw us, she backed away, in a half crouch. Adrian paused just long enough to rip the phone from the wall and toss it across the room. I followed him down the hallway, through a tidy little kitchen, where a woman in baby-doll pajamas sat at the table drinking a glass of orange juice, as though nothing unusual were happening, and out the back door and down the short steps to the alley, where Clarice waited with the Lamborghini idling. Rob was in the front seat beside her, still dead to the world. We piled into the backseat.

"Hit it," Adrian said. Clarice did.

"We ought to be okay now," I said.

"Maybe. But that wasn't the cops she was calling. They're gonna be pissed." After we were out on the street, he said, "Jesus. Did you see that old bitch move?"

"A lesson in the perils of sexism," I said. "You can't underestimate the ladies anymore."

"Women," Clarice said.

"No fuckin' shit," Adrian said. He grinned at me. "The bazooka came in handy, after all, didn't it? I'll remember that."

I shrugged. "If you hadn't come back, I'd still be standing there with my dick in my hand," I said. "We're even."

"Why is it that men always talk dirty when they're excited?" Clarice asked. But she seemed excited, too. She was whipping the car around corners, accelerating on the straightaways. Her eyes were round and bright in the rear-view mirror.

Adrian laughed. "We're a hell of a team," he said. "All three of us. Ain't that something?" He reached up and gave Clarice a pat on the shoulder. She didn't flinch this time.

We circled back to the shopping center so I could get my car, then stopped again at the edge of town, in the parking lot of a football stadium, where Adrian and I wrestled Rob Lucas into the backseat of the Celica. Clarice joined me in the front. Across the street from the football stadium was a big cemetery. It looked like, if you were sitting up in one of the top rows, watching a game, you'd be able to look right down on all the graves. Perspective, Dexter would say.

Adrian gave us a wave and tore off down the highway. I put the Celica in gear and followed at a more sedate pace.

I handed the videotapes to Clarice.

"What's this?"

"In case Rob wants a souvenir of his little holiday," I said. "The management was thoughtful enough to record it for posterity."

"Jesus."

"If it's any consolation, I doubt that there's much real action on there. Those other two are probably of somebody else."

We rode in silence most of the way back to the Lucas house, where I parked well up the drive, so we could take Rob in the side door without attracting any attention. When he was back upstairs in his bed, we went down to the living room and sat on opposite ends of the sofa.

"That's twice I owe you," Clarice said. "The campaign would be over by now if you hadn't helped us."

"I don't know," I said. "There's Nick and Uncle Dexter."

She gave me a questioning smile, but said, "Yes. It was good of them to help."

"Maybe not," I said. "I think Dexter was just protecting an investment."

"What do you mean?"

"I mean that Dexter has something to do with those pills that Rob takes. The ones that have him in a coma upstairs at this very moment."

"I don't understand. Dr. Blaine gives him those pills. They're for his headaches."

"Maybe it started that way," I said, "but it's gone way past that. He needs them now. They're taking over his life."

"But why would Dr. Blaine . . ."

"Because he works for Dexter."

"What?"

"Either that or Dexter has something on him. And I know that Blaine thinks Rob needs treatment, to get off the pills, but that Dexter wants to put that off until after the election."

"How can you know all that?"

"I know. Believe me."

She was silent for a moment. She didn't really appear surprised by anything I'd said, only saddened. At last she took a deep breath and said, "What can we do?"

"For right now, maybe not too much. Work on keeping him straight, I guess. Dexter and Blaine have an interest in keeping him propped up until the election, so they won't be fighting you."

"But after the election . . ."

"Dexter says he'll go along with treatment then, but I'm not sure he means it. If Rob kicks, then Dexter's got no leverage over him. But if Rob goes public . . ."

"Goes public?" That suggestion seemed to startle her more than anything else I'd said.

"There's a lot of that going around nowadays," I said. "Every week some celebrity goes into a clinic somewhere. People are used to it. Maybe he can get into a program at Menninger's and not even have to leave the state capital. If he can get rid of it early, it won't even be an issue in the next election. Hell, it may even work to his advantage. But the main thing is to get him out of Dexter's pocket. Even if he's clean, if he's afraid to go public with it, Dexter could still blackmail him.''

She was silent for a long time, her gaze turned inward. Finally she nodded. "I don't like it," she said. "But I see that you're right."

"It all depends on Rob," I said. "Whether he's strong enough to do it."

"He'll have to be," she said. She was trying to be tough, but I could see that something had gone out of her. I remembered what she'd said about the struggle of getting him through his wife's death, to where he was willing to campaign for office. It must look like starting all over again to her now.

"Well, anyway," I said, "it's been a fun evening."

She gave me a little smile. "Yes," she said, "I think it actually was, for you and Nick. It was as if you somehow enjoyed going in there and nearly getting killed and coming out together, the way you did. You were like a couple of kids who'd just scored a winning touchdown or something. For a second, I thought you were going to jump up and slap hands."

I laughed and shrugged. "Well," I said, "there's always a charge to that kind of thing. And we did bail each other out. It's hard not to like someone who saves your life."

"Like he said, you made a good team."

"All three of us," I said.

"I think he was only being polite about that."

"I don't know," I said. "Maybe it was me he was just being polite about."

She surprised me by laughing, then looked at me curiously. "You really didn't notice, did you?" she said.

"Notice what?"

"That our friend Nick is as queer as a three-dollar bill. I thought it was pretty obvious."

I frowned. "One of the girls back there said something like that," I said. "I thought it was just a random insult. How is it that women know these things?"

She shrugged. "I don't know. I guess it's that you expect a response that you're used to, and it's missing. There's none of the usual kind of tension. If you're . . . an attractive woman, you brace for it a little all the time without thinking about it, and then, when it's not there . . . it's like you're leaning into the wind, and the wind stops." She had a serious look on her face, thinking about what she was saying.

"What about Enright?" I asked. "Was there a wind blowing in his case?"

She gave me a startled look, followed by a low laugh. "Oh, yes," she said. "Definitely. In fact, he was something of a lech."

"And Eddie?" I said.

She nodded. "I told you I thought he had a crush on me."

I nodded sourly. Rob hadn't convinced me my homosexual theory was wrong, but I had a lot more faith in Clarice's judgment.

"I think someone has a crush on you," she added, giving me a playful smile.

I blinked at her stupidly, thinking for an off-balance moment that she was talking about herself. "Who?"

"Nick, of course."

"What?"

She laughed at my expression. "Don't worry," she said. "I think you're safe as long as you keep that gun with you."

After a moment, I laughed, too. "The funny thing is," I said, "I kind of like him."

"I won't tell anyone."

"Not that way, though," I said.

"I didn't think so." She suddenly slid over next to me and leaned her body into mine. "How do you like me?" she asked.

"Better than I do Nick," I said, my voice suddenly husky.

123

"I thought so," she said. She began unbuttoning her blouse, then paused. "You want to do this for me?"

I nodded. As my fingers tugged at the buttons, feeling twice as thick as normal, she rested one hand on my crotch and asked, "So how's the vacation going so far?"

"Better than I expected," I said. "Elk Rapids is more exciting than I thought."

"Maybe you've just been hanging out with the wrong crowd." She breathed the words in my ear, her lips nibbling at my lobe.

I had time to remember that Dexter had said something very similar to me, and to reflect that he might have been right after all. Then I was thinking about other things.

CHAPTER
TWELVE

It was still dark when I left the Lucas house, and Rob and Clarice were both sound asleep. Sometime during the night I'd decided to spend my "vacation" seeing what I could do to help them.

There were clouds coming in from the north. It was going to be a gray day, hot and sticky. The gravel lot by the motel and coffee shop was full of trucks and police cruisers and even a couple of regular cars. Dexter would be in there already, at his corner table, entertaining his cronies. The smaller lot surrounding the Blue Tattoo was empty. I parked around on the side of the little building, so my car wouldn't be visible from the coffee shop. Around in the back was a door that opened on a service stairway to Dexter's apartment. It was locked, but I knew where he hid the key that he left there for latecomers to the monthly Las Vegas nights.

As I expected, the apartment was empty. I took a quick look through the rooms, finding nothing of interest. It was the little office at the front I really wanted to check out, and the door to it from this side was unlocked, as I'd expected. There was a safe in the wall behind an enlarged photo of the place as it had looked in the 1920s, but I knew I had no hope of getting into that unless I found the combination in his desk. It was the desk where I hoped to find what I was looking for.

I did, though I didn't recognize it at first because it just looked like a rolled up tube of papers, held together by a rubber band. When I looked down the tube, however, I found a thin amber medicine bottle that turned out to contain half a dozen pills that looked just like the ones I'd taken from Rob, the night of his accident. The bottle was blank except for a thin strip of white tape with a date written on it. The date was in June, just over a year ago. It meant nothing to me.

I hesitated. Now that I'd found the pills, I wasn't quite sure what the best thing would be to do with them. It occurred to me that, because I wasn't officially a cop at the moment, just a burglar, they might actually be admissible in court, if I were willing to take the rap for the burglary and testify as to where I'd found them. I wasn't sure I was ready to go quite that far in the service of justice, but Dexter couldn't be sure of that either, if it came down to it. Anyway, I wasn't sure it was justice I was after.

The sun was nearly up when I got to the station, but Bullard's parking space was still empty, as I'd hoped. I figured Jack Molini would still be finishing up the night shift in the lab, probably dozing on one of the tables, or playing games on the Macintosh they'd bought him.

As it turned out, he had his feet up on his desk, reading a Mary Higgins Clark mystery.

"I can't believe you read that shit," I said.

"Don't knock it if you ain't tried it." He dog-eared the page he was on and waited to see what I'd brought him.

I took out my two envelopes—the big manila one with Dexter's pill bottle inside, still wrapped in its tube of paper, and the smaller one with the two pills I'd taken from Rob Lucas, and put them on Molini's desk, next to his feet. He stared at them.

126

"I heard you were off duty for a while," he said.

I nodded. "This would be a personal favor," I said. "Not official police work."

He swung his feet to the floor. "Oh, well that's no problem, then," he said. "A little free lab work for a citizen. Why not? Just so long as it's not official department business for an off-duty cop." He picked up a narrow letter opener and used it to edge the envelopes nearer to him.

"The envelopes are mine," I said. "It's the contents I want you to look at. Pills. They look alike to me, but I want to find out if they really are, and what they are. Can you do that here?"

"I expect so, long as it's not some rare tropical poison from the jungles of Paraguay."

"How soon?"

He glanced at the clock on the wall and frowned. "I'm supposed to get off in half an hour," he said.

"Sorry," I said.

He shrugged. "Either it'll be easy," he said, "and I can get it done in an hour or so, or it'll be practically impossible and I'll have to send it on to the state lab, anyway. Come back in an hour and I'll let you know."

I wasn't really expecting Dr. Blaine to be at his clinic this early, but I got lucky. He was all alone in his office, hunched over the computer terminal at his receptionist's desk, his glasses perched about halfway down his nose.

He glanced up irritably when he noticed me, and said, "The clinic's not open yet." Then he recognized me. "Oh . . . Officer Branch, isn't it? What is it? Is there a body?"

"Not today so far," I said. "But it's early yet." I sat down in one of the waiting-room chairs and slid it closer to his desk. He frowned at me. "I'm here to talk about one of your private patients," I said.

"Oh? Well, that's a little . . ."

"Rob Lucas," I said.

He closed his mouth and looked straight at me for a second. Then, speaking very slowly, as though framing each word carefully, he said, "What exactly is your interest in Mr. Lucas?"

"I've only met Mr. Lucas three or four times," I said, "but two of those times he was quite obviously under the influence of some sort of powerful drug. The second time was worse than the first time. It's my unprofessional opinion that Rob Lucas has somehow acquired a first-degree jones of some kind."

He thought about that for a long time. "And do you have a professional opinion?" he asked at last. He was trying to be glib, but it wasn't quite coming across. He was scared—more scared than I'd expected.

"You mean as an officer of the law?" I said. "Not as yet. Right now, I'm operating as a friend of the family."

He nodded, relaxing just a little, and leaned back in his chair.

"Well, then, what I can tell you . . ."

I interrupted him. "That doesn't mean you can stonewall me on this, doctor. I have samples of the pills, and my interest in them could get professional real quick."

He nodded, swallowing. "Yes. Rob told me you kept them when you found them in his car. But I think you'll find . . ."

"That he's got a prescription. He told me that. What about the ones I got from Dexter Gennaro? Does he have a prescription, too?"

That hit him where he lived. Blaine's face actually turned white, something I'd never seen happen before.

"How . . . how did you . . ."

"I borrowed them," I said. "He doesn't know they're gone. Yet."

Blaine looked away from me, wheels turning rapidly behind his eyes. "Oh sweet Jesus," he said. "He'll think . . ."

"That you took them?" I asked. "That's interesting." That hadn't occurred to me, but it made sense.

Blaine licked his lips. He seemed to be having some trouble getting his breath. He fumbled inside his jacket, and I tensed, but he came out with a little pill case of his own. He opened it and took out two tiny white pills, popping them into his mouth and swallowing them dry. After a moment, he seemed to get his breath and some of his color back.

"What . . . what are you going to do?" he asked, his voice husky.

"That depends," I said. "At the moment, I'm just interested in helping Rob get clear of Dexter. I figure Dexter has some kind of hold over you and I want to know what it is, and just what the two of you have been up to. I'm not particularly interested in putting you in jail if I can avoid it."

He thought about it, his eyes unfocused. "Fifteen years," he said absently. Then his expression cleared and he looked at me. "All right," he said. "It started out as a treatment for migraine. Rob has severe, incapacitating attacks every six months or so. He also puts a lot of stress on himself, of course, and that probably contributes. Anyway, in the last year or so the frequency of the attacks has been increasing . . . or at least he's been filling the prescription a lot more often. As you've observed, his behavior is getting out of control. Believe me, I'm as interested as you are in getting him straightened out."

"But Dexter isn't," I said.

He sighed and looked down at his hands, which were twisted together on the desk top. "I owe Dexter some money," he said. "A lot of money. There was a malpractice suit, involving . . . well, the details aren't important. But I would have lost, and it would have wiped me out, both financially and professionally. Dexter bankrolled a settlement, kept it out of court. He even squared it with the insurance company somehow, so they didn't cancel me. At the time, I was just grateful. I didn't realize what he'd want in return."

"It goes beyond Rob," I said.

He nodded, still studying his fingers. "In fact, it had nothing to do with Rob initially," he said. "That just happened. At first, it was just drugs . . . recreational drugs, they call them nowadays. . . ." He gave a sharp, bitter laugh. "For Dexter's friends," he said.

"Rich friends," I said.

He shrugged. "Dexter likes doing things for people, having them owe him things."

I wondered how far that extended, who else there might be who owed Dexter something, who might be interested in helping him keep things quiet. I filed the thought away for future reference. "What does all this have to do with the Enright case?" I asked Blaine.

He blinked at me in surprise. "Enright? Oh, you mean Bill Elmore?" He shook his head. "Nothing at all, that I know of." He sighed. "It's amazing, isn't it? He was leading a completely secret life. Nobody knew who he really was."

"Maybe somebody did," I said.

He looked at me from behind the little square spectacles, but didn't say anything. He seemed to be getting his equanimity back, after the initial scare.

"Seems to me there are a number of people leading secret lives in this town," I said.

He started to say something, then just nodded and looked back down at his hands.

I told Blaine to stay available, and went back to the police station, slipping in through a back door and getting to Molini's lab without seeing anyone. He had the two sets of pills arranged neatly on the table in front of him and was staring at them, his hands folded across his stomach.

"That how you do it?" I asked. "Stare at them until the answer forms in your brain?"

He gave me a halfhearted smile. "Where'd you get these?" he asked.

"I can't tell you yet," I said. "I'm sorry."

He nodded, obviously not pleased with that answer. "This isn't the kind of thing we ought to be sitting on," he said.

"What is it?"

He pursed his lips and lifted one hand to point at the pills I'd taken from Rob Lucas. "These," he said, "contain a mixture of things, but the main ingredient is a member of the methadone family called dextromoramide. It's about twice as powerful as morphine, and three or four times as addictive."

I whistled. "This is the stuff they developed as an alternative for heroin addicts," I said.

He nodded. "There's a school of thought that it's easier to function normally when you're hooked on this stuff, than when you're hooked on heroin. Also, it's supposed to be administered by a physician, as formal treatment. It's not supposed to be floating around loose, out in the general population."

"Noted," I said. "The others the same?"

He frowned. "Not quite. There's one added ingredient in those."

"What's that?"

"Cyanide."

"Cyanide," I repeated stupidly. It wasn't at all the kind of answer I'd been expecting. Some of the pieces that had started to look like they might fit began pulling apart again in my mind. "Deadly," I said.

"Oh, yes. Pop a couple of these and you'll feel real good for about five minutes, and then you'll fall right over on your face."

That image rang a bell in my memory. "Would it look like a heart attack?" I asked.

He frowned at me. "Well . . . not if you did an autopsy. But to someone just standing there when it happened . . . sure."

"What about a doctor?" I asked. "Could a doctor be fooled?"

"Doubtful. Cyanide corpses have a distinctive look. The skin turns bluish. Not the same as a cardiac condition."

I managed to fend off Molini's questions and get away, but apparently I hadn't gotten in as smoothly as I'd thought, because Mike Farrar was waiting outside the lab for me, leaning against the wall with his hands in his pockets.

"Let's go get some coffee somewhere," he said. He didn't seem very happy. He looked like he'd been wearing the same gray suit for a couple of days, and his white hair stuck up on both sides of his head like undersized angel wings.

We got in my car and I drove to a pancake place I knew he liked where they had high-backed booths and the clientele was mostly traveling salesmen and the occasional farmer. Mike didn't say anything during the ride, just stared out the side window with his arms folded.

"You're still at it," he said, once we'd gotten our coffee and the waitress had left us alone.

"Not the Enright case," I said. "This is something else."

He studied me for a moment, then said, "You want to tell me what you had Molini looking at?"

"Sure." I went over it from the top, beginning with Rob's accident and the pills I'd taken from him. I admitted the break-in at Dexter's place, which made him wince, and told him about my conversation with Blaine, the connection between Blaine and Dexter, and the stuff Blaine was prescribing for Rob. I told him I thought Rob was probably in the clear, legally. I didn't mention my suspicions about Bullard's connection with Dexter, because I had no idea where Mike might stand on that. When it came to the cyanide, I hesitated, then went ahead and told him about that, too, figuring he could find out anyway by asking Molini. I didn't tell him what I was thinking about it, though, because I hadn't quite finished thinking about it yet.

"Cyanide," he said. "Do you remember any unsolved poisonings?"

I shook my head. "So," I said, "you mind telling me what's happening in the Enright case? The hundred grand turn up yet?"

He gave a twisted smile. "You know I ain't supposed to talk to you about that," he said. Then he shrugged. "But what the shit. That's between you and Bullard, far as I'm concerned." He took a sip of coffee and said, "The FBI guys blew in yesterday and spent most of the day with Bullard. There was some shouting."

I smiled. "They think maybe it could have disappeared during the investigation?"

Mike gave me a surprised look. "You thought of that, too?" he asked.

"I know how they think. Every local cop is on the take, as far as those assholes are concerned. Trouble is, they're too often right."

Mike grunted. "Looking for the money is about all we're doing now," he said. "We're trying to backtrack Eddie, figure out where he could have stashed it. Bullard thinks that's the key." He shrugged. "Maybe he's right. I got no better plan."

"I'm not sure I do, either," I said. "Offhand, I can't see how this drug thing and the killings are connected."

"No. Just like the money, all it does is fuck things up more." He took another sip of his coffee and made a face as though the taste had turned bad. "It just keeps gettin' worse and worse," he said.

I wasn't entirely sure what he was talking about, so I didn't say anything. He looked away from me, out the window beside our booth, his face drained, slack. He'd always looked old to me, but for a second he looked old and sick, like someone who ought to be home in bed, not out chasing around after murderers.

"You okay?" I asked.

He glanced at me distractedly, as though he hadn't heard what I'd said. Then his eyes cleared and he said, "Oh, yeah. I'm fine. I'm just havin' a little trouble sleepin' lately."

"The heat?"

He shrugged.

"The Skubitz kid," I said. "That's still bothering you."

He gave the smallest of nods, a barely perceptible movement of his head.

"It wasn't your fault," I told him.

He looked at me, squinting slightly, as though trying to make sense out of what I'd just said. "Did you know," he said finally, "that I grew up out there by Randall Drive? I knew those kids' grandparents. Me and Andy Skubitz went off to Korea at the same time. He didn't come back." His gaze drifted off into reminiscence, and he was silent for a while. I sipped my coffee and didn't say anything. After a moment, he shrugged. "Not that we were best friends or anything," he said. "He was just someone I knew. But what if I'd died in Korea and Andy'd come back? Everything would be completely different now for everybody." He gave a choked laugh. "You ever think about things like that?" he asked.

"Oh, yes," I said. "I do."

Mike stood up and fumbled in his pocket for a tip. "I gotta get out of here," he said. I knew he wasn't just talking about the café.

As I'd expected, it had turned into a gray, muggy day. I ran the air conditioner in the car, driving Mike back to the station, but it seemed to do little good. I felt grimy all over by the time I drove back to the clinic, to ask Blaine about the cyanide. His car wasn't there anymore, and his receptionist didn't know where he was. I left a message for him to call me. As I was leaving, I thought I spotted a black Lamborghini sitting against the curb a half block away. I cruised by the staff parking lot at the hospital, but Blaine wasn't there, either. I stopped at a gas station nearby that had a pay phone with a phone book dangling from it and looked up Blaine's home address. When I pulled back out, I saw the Lamborghini pull out, too, a block behind.

Instead of driving to Blaine's house, I headed for home, keeping an eye on the rearview mirror. Once it became obvious where I was going, Adrian closed up to a car-length behind me, obviously not caring whether I noticed him or not.

When I pulled up at the curb in front of my place, he pulled in right behind me and got out, smiling, looking neat and cool in the heat.

"Hey, good buddy," he said. "How's the vacation going?"

"Hi, Nick," I said. "You off duty, too? Just cruising around town, showing off your wheels?"

He shook his head regretfully. "Nope. Working. Fact is, Dexter sent me to tell you he'd like to talk to you."

"He could have phoned. I have an answering machine."

"I guess he wanted you to know how important it is to him. You know, if he just called, you could blow him off, pretend you never got the message."

"I could decide to blow him off, anyway," I said. We were both smiling, leaning against my car, as though chatting about how the Royals were doing.

Nick nodded. "You could do that," he said, "and then I'd have to insist." He glanced at my jacket. "I can see you don't have the cannon with you," he said.

"But you've got your own little friend, I'll bet," I said.

He grinned. "I don't need to show it to you, do I?"

"Well," I said, "it's always such a thrill to see it."

"I know, but it might alarm the neighbors."

I nodded. "Good point. Shall I follow you?"

He smiled more broadly. "That's great," he said. "I didn't really want to have to insist. I still feel like I owe you for the guy at the whorehouse. I would have, you understand. It's my job. But I wouldn't like it."

"Well," I said, "nobody should have to do a job they don't like."

CHAPTER
THIRTEEN

"How long you been tailing me?" I asked Nick when we got out of our cars at the truckstop.

"I picked you up outside the clinic this morning," he said. "Dexter sent me there to get Doc Blaine, but I saw you go in, so I gave Dexter a call, and he said to forget about the doc and follow you. So I did. To the police station, then out to that second-rate diner with the other cop. You sure lead an exciting life. While you were there, I called Dexter again and he told me to wait till you went home, then bring you out here."

"Just like that."

Nick grinned. "Dexter has a lot of faith in my persuasive powers," he said.

"So you never picked up Dr. Blaine?"

He shook his head. "You were looking for him, huh? That's why the hospital and all. Guess he's split." He shrugged. He didn't seem to care much, one way or the other.

Dexter was in the big office at the motel. His secretary, a little round lady who reminded me of Mrs. Jackson, gave Nick a motherly smile as he escorted me past her. Dexter was leaning back in his wooden swivel chair, his arms behind his head.

"I talked to Pat Bullard," he said. "He tells me you're suspended."

"That's right. He tell you why?"

"Not in any detail. Something to do with a disagreement about the murder investigation, I gather."

"That's what I thought, too," I said.

Dexter gave me a speculative look. "Well, anyway," he said, "I'm sorry to hear it."

"That why you had Nick drag me out here?"

"No. Of course not." He chewed for a moment at his lower lip, then said, "You visited Dr. Blaine this morning. Before his clinic opened."

"I admit it," I said.

"Then you went to the police station, even though you're off duty, and you visited the lab."

I gave Nick an approving glance. He shrugged and grinned.

"What I think," Dexter said carefully, "is that Dr. Blaine may have given you something, which you took in to have analyzed."

I understood then that he didn't know about my earlier visit to the lab. He was giving me an earnest look, wanting me to say yes or no.

"I'm curious," I said. "When you talked to Bullard about me, did you tell him all this—about my visit to Blaine and to the lab, and what you thought about it all?"

Dexter smiled pleasantly. "No," he said. "I didn't."

"You just called him up out of the blue and asked him what Lt. Johnny Branch was working on these days. And he told you I was suspended."

"Well . . . it wasn't quite like that. I called him about something else, and your name came up and I mentioned that I'd heard you were on vacation, and he confided to me that he'd actually suspended you for a while. He wasn't too happy about it, by the way, but he seemed to think it was necessary."

I nodded. "You want to know about my business with Blaine," I said. "And I'd like to know about your business with Blaine. Interested in trading?"

Dexter glanced at Adrian. "Nick," he said, "why don't you go get some lunch. I won't be needing you here for a while."

Nick went out without a sound, closing the door behind him. Dexter looked up at me, waiting.

"Okay," I said. "I'll go first. But I don't think you're going to like it. First of all, Blaine didn't give me anything. I just went to see him to talk about Rob Lucas. I went to the police lab to get a report on some pills I'd taken from Lucas a week or so ago, when he was in an auto accident and obviously under the influence of something." It was all true— just a couple of things left out. I expected Dexter would leave some things out of whatever it was he was going to tell me.

"I see," Dexter said, "and why the sudden interest in Rob Lucas?"

I shrugged and gave him my best boyish grin. "I guess I'd have to say it's more of a sudden interest in Clarice Lucas."

I expected a grin in return, but instead I got a frown. "You're involved with her?" Dexter asked.

"Maybe. Why would you care?"

He shook his head, his expression clearing. "It's just something I hadn't considered," he said. "As I told you before, I think of Rob and Clarice as . . . sort of a nephew and niece. But of course Clarice is a grown woman."

"She's definitely that," I said.

He gave me a quick little look of dislike which he just as quickly covered with a polite smile. "And then there's Marcie Skubitz," he said. "What about her?"

"You're the one who suggested I make new friends."

He gave a soft, mirthless laugh and nodded. "So I did. So I did." He seemed to consider that for a moment, then said, "But concerning Rob . . ."

"Rob hasn't been well served by his doctor," I said. "Or by his 'uncle,' either, apparently."

"You mean me. What do you think I have to do with it?"

I hesitated, then said, "I already know Blaine owes you money and you're using that as leverage to make sure Rob keeps getting the pills. I'm not entirely sure what you get out of it, but I'd guess it's an investment for political favors, down the line."

"Blaine told you that?"

"Not that last part."

Dexter thought about that for a while. He didn't seem either surprised or particularly disturbed. "So, assuming this is true," he said at last, "what do you plan to do?"

"As I told Blaine," I said, "at this point I'm just a friend of the family. I'm interested in helping get Rob unhooked. I've told Clarice what's going on, and I've told her that after the election Rob needs to get both you and the drugs off his back, even if it means going public with his problem."

I thought that would get Dexter's attention, and it did. He stared at me like someone hearing a fascinating story he'd never heard before. "And how did Clarice take that?" he asked.

"She didn't like it, but she finally agreed I was right."

He nodded. "And why are you telling me all this?" he asked.

I shrugged. "Because we're trading, remember? I want to find out just how much of a problem you're going to be for Rob."

He smiled. "Not much of one," he said softly. "You obviously have me pegged as the bad guy in this, but the fact is I really am as concerned about Rob as you are. I have no interest in turning him into a junkie. In fact, that process was well along before I ever came into the picture. I agree with you completely—about getting treatment after the election, I mean. I don't see the need to go public with it—he certainly doesn't have to do that because of me—but I see your reasoning. The question is, will he be able to do it?"

"With Clarice behind him, and no one standing in his way, I think he can," I said.

Dexter nodded doubtfully. "Perhaps you're right," he said. "At any rate, I won't be the one standing in his way."

It wasn't going quite as I'd expected, but I tried not to show it. "Your turn," I said.

He was silent for a moment, his head slightly bent, as though studying the papers on his desk. Then he gave a small nod and looked up at me.

"I've decided to be completely honest with you," he said, "because I think you and I can have that kind of relationship. You're interested in my relationship with Pat Bullard, and that's understandable, since you're likely to be chief yourself someday." He paused. If he was waiting for a reaction from me, he didn't get one. After a moment, he went on. "You've been around enough to know that any community—a big one like Kansas City or a small one like Elk Rapids—is really run by a . . . a power structure, I guess you'd call it." He seemed to like the phrase, and repeated it. "A power structure. A group of . . . community leaders—not all of them elected, but still . . . people whose interest in the community runs deep, who are in a position to exert what influence they have on behalf of the community."

"Or in their own behalf," I said.

Dexter blinked at me and then nodded. "Of course, there are abuses of power," he said. "It's not the way the system is supposed to work, according to the textbooks, but it's the way the system does work, the way it's always really worked. That's just a fact. Everyone can choose to work with it or against it. That's the choice we're all faced with, at some point—myself as well as you. I didn't invent the situation. In fact, there was a time, not that long ago, when I was very much against it, when the people who really ran this community didn't consider people like me a part of it. In those days, if you had a name like Gennaro, you worked in the mines or you went elsewhere. Those were your choices.'' He smiled as if in fond remembrance. ''But those days are gone,'' he said with satisfaction. ''And I've had a part in changing things. Not by fighting the system, but by working with it until some of us who had been outsiders were in position to start calling the shots ourselves. What we've got now isn't perfect, but it's better than it was—and not just for a handful of families who live on Circle Street.'' He gave me a challenging look, his chin slightly raised.

''Okay,'' I said, ''I get it. The police chief has to fit in to that if he wants to get anything done. You're right. It's that way everywhere. My question is, how far does it go? There have to be limits. They may be hard to see, but they're there. Sometimes the only way you can see them is by seeing what goes beyond them. Like drugs.''

''You mean illegal drugs,'' Dexter said. ''Heroin, crack, that kind of thing.''

''Any drug can be illegal,'' I said.

''That's right,'' Dexter said, with sudden force. ''And by the same token, nearly any drug can be legal. It's a matter of circumstances. Of course, there are some drugs, like the ones I mentioned, that are always illegal. Mere possession is illegal, no matter how you got them. But others . . .''

''Are you trying to tell me you have prescriptions for all the drugs Blaine has given you?'' I asked.

Dexter smiled. ''Let me ask you a question,'' he said. ''If you go to your doctor and, instead of writing you a prescription and sending you to the drugstore, he hands you a sample packet he's gotten from one of the drug companies and says, 'Here, try these. They're supposed to be effective for what you've got,' and you take them—are you in violation of the law?''

I thought about it and shook my head. In fact, I remembered having gotten medicine that way once or twice.

''Okay,'' Dexter said. ''Now let's say that your wife—or

even just a good friend—comes to you and says, 'Boy, I'm feeling lousy,' and it turns out they've got the same thing you had, and the drugs the doctor gave you made you feel better, and so you slip a couple of them to your friend. Is either one of you in violation of the law?''

"You shouldn't . . .'' I began.

"I'm not saying, is it a good idea,'' Dexter said. "I'm perfectly willing to grant that no one should be taking medicine that hasn't been prescribed for him. I wouldn't do it myself. But then, I don't smoke, either, and I don't think people are wise to do so. But I sell cigarettes downstairs. The question is, is anyone breaking a law?''

"No money changes hands?'' I asked.

"Not a dime.''

I shook my head reluctantly. "But that's not really the situation we're talking about here,'' I said.

"Isn't it? You might be surprised. I have a number of friends who lead very stressful lives, who like to find ways to relax, and I like to help them, as much as I can. Dr. Blaine, like all doctors, receives samples of new drugs from perfectly respectable drug companies and he tries them out sometimes on his patients. Possession of such drugs isn't illegal, nor is giving them to someone else. And sometimes I do pass them on—as gifts, to special friends of mine. I admit it may be unwise. Sometimes I regret it. But I don't think you'll find a DA willing to go to court about it.''

"I didn't get the impression that Blaine was talking about a handful of sample drugs,'' I said. "It sounded like he was talking about a substantial volume and a regular rate.''

Dexter shrugged. "You'd be surprised how much stuff of that kind doctors receive,'' he said. "Most of it they throw away, I suppose.''

"And what about the money Blaine owes you?'' I asked. "If he's using drugs to pay off a debt . . .''

"He may think he is,'' Dexter says. "Maybe what he's doing is illegal, from that perspective. But I certainly don't

143

regard the drugs in that light. If we were in court, I could prove that the debt hasn't been reduced. Blaine may think he's being coerced into handing over the drugs, but . . . well, again, that's his perspective. The question is, what would a jury believe? That's what it all comes down to, doesn't it? And whether it's worth anyone's time to find out. You know about those Las Vegas nights I host over at my place. Those are clearly illegal under Kansas law—so is making a bet with a friend, for that matter—but Pat Bullard has made a decision that no one is actually being harmed, and it's not really worth his department's time to worry about it. Isn't that so?''

I nodded. ''And what does he get out of it?'' I asked.

Dexter blinked in surprise. ''You mean Bullard, person-ally? Nothing. It's not that kind of thing, Johnny. You have a wrong idea about us. What Bullard gets is friendship and cooperation and support from the people whose support means something arond here. If he wants to buy some new equipment—or hire an ex-vice detective from Kansas City—nobody gives him any trouble about it. The money's in the budget. The decision is his.''

''It all just keeps the wheels greased,'' I said.

''That's it. It's the same everywhere. We're not talking about graft. I hope you understand that. We're talking about . . .'' he paused and then smiled more broadly. ''Home rule,'' he said. ''We're talking about a community setting its own standards and taking care of its own. That's all.''

I didn't say anything for a moment. I knew Dexter's ar-gument wouldn't hold up if I took the time to put it under a microscope, but that wasn't what bothered me. Rather, it was a sense I had of something else I was missing—something I ought to be seeing and wasn't, something that scared me. Was Dexter just the good old boy he appeared to be, spouting the same old hokum, or was it some kind of smoke screen? Was Dexter that smart? Down inside me, like a toothache that I'd just noticed but that had been there for a long time, was the old panicky feeling, the apprehension that nothing was as it seemed, that I could no longer trust my own judgment or perceptions. I had brought that feeling with me from Kansas City, and it was still there. Maybe Bullard was right about me. The only way I could find out, it seemed to me, was to follow the things I knew, to make the connections.

"Betty June Lucas," I said. "Was she a friend of yours?"

Dexter's smile faded for just a second, then turned into a look of polite regret. "Of course she was," he said. "Why do you ask?"

I shook my head. "Something Dr. Blaine said. That Rob's drug use had increased in the past year. And it was just about a year ago that Betty June died." I named the date—the date that was on the bottle I'd taken from Dexter's desk. "That was it, wasn't it? The night of the party where she died?"

He licked his lips, as rattled as I'd ever seen him, and said, "That sounds right. I wasn't there."

I stared at him for a moment, and he looked back at me, not speaking.

"Well," I said at last, "it occurred to me, if Rob's increased drug use started after Betty June's death, it might be more than grief. It might be guilt. Maybe because he knew she took something that night that wasn't good for her—because of her bad heart, I mean." I gave Dexter a questioning look, trying to look like the bright kid who thought he'd figured everything out.

I got the reaction I'd hoped for: a look of relief, followed by an expression of concern.

"You mean the drugs I've given some of my friends," Dexter said. "I'd hate to think that was true. But the thing is, I've never given any of those drugs to Rob, if that's what you're thinking. So I don't think Rob would have any reason to feel guilty."

"And what about you?"

"Me?" He acted as though he were thinking about it. Maybe he was. "If something I gave someone contributed to Betty June Lucas's death, I'd certainly regret it," he said at last. "But it would be an accident—a tragic accident." He shook his head. "But the same thing could have been caused by alcohol, I suppose, and . . . suppose you'd fixed her a drink at that party and then she'd died. Would you feel guilt? Maybe a little, for a short while. But these things happen. No one knew she had a heart condition."

I nodded, thinking for a moment myself of how guilt attaches, of what innocence requires, of how often it seemed to be the things that weren't known about people that got them killed. Not only Betty June Lucas, but Doolie Waters, Walter Enright, maybe even Eddie Skubitz.

"Is there some new interest in the death of Mrs. Lucas?" Dexter asked carefully.

I shook my head. "Not that I know of," I said. "I'm mainly concerned about Rob and Clarice, that's all."

"And what about the other matters we've discussed?"

"The drugs?" I shrugged. I knew Dexter wasn't telling me the whole truth there, but it wasn't something I wanted to worry about right now. I found that I believed what he'd said about Rob. "I understand your perspective," I told him. "And Bullard's."

"That's good," Dexter said. "I'm glad we had this talk. It clears the air between us." He reached for a phone on his desk. "I'll have Nick drive you back."

"Don't bother. I came in my own car."

He blinked. That appeared to surprise him as much as anything else I'd said. I guessed there were things he didn't know about Nick, too. Dexter stood and held out his hand and I shook it.

Downstairs, Nick was leaning against the bar, nursing a drink. When he saw me come down, he sidled over.

"Everything okay, I hope," he said.

"Hunky-dory," I said.

"Glad to hear it. Buy you a drink?"

"Some other time," I said.

"Anytime," he said. "Anytime at all." He went back to the bar.

If Dexter believed me, which he seemed to, it meant Blaine was still his number one suspect in the disappearance of the cyanide pills, so I figured I'd better find Blaine before Nick did. Also, I still wanted to ask him about the cyanide. I swung by the clinic and the hospital again, without success, then went to his house, making sure I wasn't being followed. The driveway was empty, but the garage was locked up and I couldn't see inside. When I rang the bell, nothing happened, so I leaned on it for a while. No matter how determined you are not to receive guests, it's almost impossible to ignore a ringing bell for more than a minute or so. Nevertheless, I'd given up and was heading back down the sidewalk to my car when I heard the door open behind me. A very large woman in a dark blue housedress stood there, clutching a Bible against her chest. I walked back.

"Mrs. Blaine?" I said.

She nodded, eyeing me suspiciously.

"Is Dr. Blaine in?"

She shook her head. "You'll have to call his office to make an appointment," she said.

"It's not medical," I said. "It's personal. Very important that I see him."

"He's not here," she said.

"Do you know where I could find him?"

She shook her head.

I hesitated. I would have shown her my badge, except I didn't have it. I realized that without it it would be more difficult than usual to talk my way inside. I settled for giving her a card from my wallet.

She glanced at it, apparently unimpressed, and made no move to invite me in.

After a silent moment during which I considered all the possibilities, including strong-arming my way in, and dis-

147

missed them all, I said, "When you see Dr. Blaine, please tell him to get in touch with me. Tell him it's very important."

She looked at me for a moment longer, giving no sign of agreement or disagreement, then closed the door.

I went to the clerk's office at the county courthouse and confirmed what I suspected, that there'd been no autopsy performed on Betty June Lucas—that Blaine had signed the death warrant, naming congenital heart defect as the cause, but giving no real grounds for that finding. Looking through the death warrants got me thinking. I walked across the alley to the police station, but Bullard was standing by the front desk, and I'd have had to go past him to get to the dayroom, where the files were kept.

Instead, I walked across the street and ate supper at the greasy spoon that had most likely prepared Eddie Skubitz's final, uneaten breakfast. Dusk was approaching outside, and the neon lights were coming on along Main Street—mostly liquor stores and pawnshops in this part of town. The only dark spot in the block across the street was the big marquee of the Princess Theater, which had been put out of business by cable TV. The letters on the marquee said "T MPO A ILY CLOS." They'd been up there for nearly six months, and the missing letters had disappeared all at once one weekend. There'd been a lot of speculation about what someone could have needed two *R*'s, two *E*'s and a *D* for, but no one had ever figured it out, and they'd never turned up anywhere.

I sat and drank coffee, gradually getting on the waitress's nerves, until I saw Bullard's car come out of the alley from the parking lot and drive away. Then I went back across the street and slipped into the dayroom, finding the files I wanted and taking them to an interrogation room that was seldom used.

Somewhat to my surprise, it turned out that Blaine hadn't been involved in either the Enright or Dixon autopsies, though he had performed the autopsy on Eddie Skubitz. Death by strangulation, it said. I shrugged and put the folders in the basket for the clerks to refile.

I took another swing past Blaine's house, but there was still no car, and no lights on anywhere. I thought about having a look in the garage, if I could figure a way, but then decided to wait awhile. I went back to the apartment, had a beer, and set my alarm clock for 3 A.M., thinking maybe I could become a burglar if the police job didn't work out.

What woke me up, however, wasn't the alarm clock but the phone. It was Dexter.

"I've got to see you again," he said. He sounded very serious.

I looked at the clock. It was nearly 2:30.

"Can't it wait till morning?" I said. "I'm not at my best right now."

There was a pause and I had the impression he was talking to someone else, probably Nick, but the sound was muffled.

"It's got to be now," he said. "It's very important. It . . . it has to do with the Enright murder."

That woke me up a bit. "Be there in fifteen minutes," I said.

It was a warm night, but there was a breeze moving through the empty streets, rattling papers in the gutters. In the stretch of road between the edge of town and Dexter's place, cicadas hammered in the trees, running down all at once now and then, like an engine being turned off. The Blue Tattoo was dark, but Rob's white Chrysler was sitting in front of the door. The rest of the lot was empty. I parked around on the side and went in through the unlocked front door. The lights were on in the stairwell and the hall, but the place felt deserted. I was nearly to the top of the stairs when Rob Lucas appeared at the top, looking nearly as white as his car.

"Branch," he said. "Thank God. I think someone's been shot."

I went on up and then past him down the corridor. The door to Dexter's office was closed. I stood back away from it and spoke to Lucas in a low voice. "Have you been in there?"

He shook his head, looking scared. I reflected that the only time I'd seen him looking completely well was in his office at the newspaper. "I just got here," he said. "I knocked on the door, and then . . . there were gunshots. I was afraid to go in."

"How long ago?" I asked.

"I don't know. No more than a couple of minutes, probably. It seemed like . . . I stood out here forever before I heard you coming up the stairs. I was afraid."

I took out my .357 and held it in my right hand while I put my left on the doorknob and took a deep breath. "Stay back against the wall," I told Lucas.

I took another breath and turned the handle. There was no resistance. I flung the door inward and rolled through it low, coming up in a squat, the gun in both hands in front of my face. I pivoted in three directions, scanning the room.

There was no one in sight, but I could see a shoe sticking out from behind one side of Dexter's desk.

I duck-walked around the side of the desk and then spread out on my belly and looked around the corner. Dexter lay on his side with his knees pulled up slightly. His swivel chair had been knocked to one side, and was pointed toward the wall. I stood up and took a closer look. He had two bullet holes in the back of his head, and blood was still spreading out around him. He hadn't been dead long, but he'd be dead forever.

CHAPTER
FOURTEEN

Rob had been looking for Dr. Blaine, too. He was nearly out of pills and his prescription needed to be renewed. According to what he told Mike Farrar, the Blue Tattoo had been the seventh or eighth place he'd tried, getting desperate. He claimed he'd had no particular reason to think Blaine might be there. He'd found the front door unlocked, and had seen the light on under Dexter's office door, so he'd knocked.

"And that's when you heard the gunshots?" Mike asked.

Rob started to nod, then looked up at me in surprise. "No," he said. "First . . . he said your name."

"What?"

"Dexter. He said, 'Branch?' Like he thought it was you knocking."

I'd already told Mike about Dexter calling me.

"So then what?" Mike asked Rob.

"I said, 'It's me. Rob.' And then . . . I was expecting him to say come on in, you know, but nothing happened. So . . . I just waited, you know? But it got to be kind of a long time, and so I was going to go in anyway. I . . . uhh . . . I reached for the knob, and that's when . . . the shots came."

"Exactly two?"

"I think so. More than one, anyway. My first thought was that he was shooting at me, through the door. I don't know why I thought that. Just . . . I guess your mind just tries to make sense of things. The next thing I knew I was halfway down the hall, up against the wall. Just flat against it, holding my breath. But then nothing else happened.''

"You didn't go back and take a look?'' Mike asked.

Rob gave a weak smile. "I couldn't make myself do it,'' he said.

"No reason you should have,'' Mike said. "The killer could have still been in there.''

"I know. But I still feel funny about it. Being that scared.'' He shook his head. "Anyway, then I heard footsteps on the stairs and I went and looked, and it was Detective Branch.''

"Just Branch these days,'' I said.

Rob gave me a politely inquisitive look, but didn't say anything.

"Thanks, Mr. Lucas,'' Mike said. "You can go on home now. If I think of anything else, I'll drop by later.''

Lucas nodded and let out a long breath, then turned and went down the stairs, keeping one hand on the railing.

"You know what it sounds like,'' Mike said to me, when he'd gone.

I nodded. "Someone wanted me and Dexter both. When Rob showed up, whoever it was decided to settle for Dexter and then split.''

"Who do you know that would want both you and Dexter dead?''

"The only one I can think of is Blaine, after the way I sweated him about the pills,'' I said.

"Yeah, that's what I was thinking, too. You find out anything about the cyanide?''

"Just that the date on the bottle was the date Betty June Lucas died, and that it was Blaine who signed the death warrant. Natural causes. No autopsy.''

"Jesus,'' Mike said. "It gets shittier and shittier.'' He frowned for a moment. "Bullard's on the way,'' he said. "Maybe you ought to clear out for now.''

I nodded.

"What you planning to do?" Mike asked.

"Look for Blaine."

"Good. Let me know if you find him?"

"Sure."

Jack Molini came out of Dexter's office with a little plastic bag.

"Anything?" Mike asked.

"Small caliber," Molini said. "I'd guess a .22. Twice in the back of the head. Looks like he was standing up behind his desk and the shooter was behind him, with the gun pointed slightly up. I'll know more in a couple of hours."

"Left- or right-handed shooter?" I asked.

Molini laughed. "You been watching too much TV," he said.

"I wonder where Nick Adrian is," I said. "I wonder why he wasn't here to protect Dexter."

"Maybe he was the shooter."

I shook my head. "He favors a knife."

"But if he was expecting to have to deal with two guys," Mike suggested.

"He wouldn't work it that way," I said. "He'd do us one at a time. Anyway, I don't see why he'd want to kill either of us."

"Just a thought. Looks like it was someone Dexter wasn't afraid of."

"That would fit Blaine," I said.

"That'd fit most of Elk Rapids," Mike said unhappily.

I drove straight to Blaine's house and parked on a side street a block away, then went up the alley. As I'd hoped, there was a back door to the garage, and I was able to force the old lock. Blaine's car was inside.

The house itself was even easier. People don't lock their doors in Elk Rapids. Wooden steps led up past a slanted cellar entrance to a door that opened into the kitchen. Inside, everything was dark and quiet. I moved slowly into the dining room, walking as softly as I could. My steps made the cups and saucers in the glass-fronted china closet shiver and tinkle, but I didn't think it was loud enough for anyone outside the room to hear. At the other end of the dining room was an arched opening leading to the living room, and beyond that, between it and the front entrance hall, there was a stairway going up. The stairs creaked, but there was no way to avoid it. I went up as quickly and quietly as I could, and then stopped at the top, listening.

What I heard was a kind of mumble, a woman's voice, low and uninflected, but with a rhythm to it, like a chant. I thought it was coming from the room just across the hall from me, but when I moved toward it, I realized it came from farther away. Gradually, I made my way to the end of the little hall, where there was a little bedroom with a gabled ceiling—a child's bedroom, it looked like. The wallpaper had horses and cowboys on it, and the base of the lamp beside the bed was a palomino stallion, rearing on its hind legs. Mrs. Blaine sat in a rocking chair beside the bed with her Bible open in her lap, reading aloud, and Dr. Blaine lay in the bed, his eyes closed, looking ancient and shriveled.

Mrs. Blaine looked up at me as I appeared in the doorway, and closed her book calmly, keeping a finger at her place.

"What do you want?" she asked in a low voice.

"I need to talk to him," I said, also speaking softly.

"I'm sorry. He's very ill." We might have been in a hospital sickroom.

Actually, he looked dead. But just then he opened his eyes and looked at me, gave a small sigh, and closed them again.

"Mrs. Blaine," I said, speaking in a more normal voice, "I'm very sorry to bother you at a time like this, but the fact is there's been a murder." Blaine's eyes opened again. "And Dr. Blaine is a suspect," I went on. "Whether or not he talks to me now, he's going to be talking to official investigators shortly."

She started to say something, but Blaine made a sound and she looked at him. "Want . . ." he said, his voice breathy.

We both leaned closer to him.

"Want to confess," he said, more steadily.

Mrs. Blaine and I looked at each other. "He's entitled to an attorney," she said calmly. I reflected that she might be the toughest person I'd met so far in Elk Rapids.

"I'm not a cop at the moment," I told her. I looked at him. "You killed Dexter?" I asked.

His eyes widened. "Dexter?"

"Somebody shot him a couple of hours ago."

"A couple of hours?" Mrs. Blaine said. "The doctor has been here in this bed since yesterday afternoon. Most of that time he wasn't conscious." She half rose from her rocking chair and pulled back one edge of the blanket to reveal the broad white bandages wrapped around Blaine's skinny wrist.

"What's that?" I asked, pointing to a small bandage higher up on his arm.

"IV," she said. "He lost enough blood to require a transfusion."

"You did that?"

"I had help. If it's necessary, they'll testify. Otherwise, I'm not saying who."

I nodded. "I believe you," I said. "But I still need to talk to him."

"I'm afraid that won't . . ."

"Eloise," he said.

She looked at him. She was a strong woman, but when he spoke, no matter how softly, she shut up.

"It's all right," he said.

She looked doubtful, her mouth tightening to a thin straight line. He gave a firm little nod, an echo of his normal authority as a doctor.

She nodded in response. "But not long," she said in a harsh whisper, reasserting some of her own nurse's authority.

I stepped back slightly, giving her room to move past me. She went out and closed the door behind her.

"She's a good woman," Blaine said. His voice was clear, though not strong.

"I'm positive of it," I said.

He licked his lips, which were dry and cracked. There was a glass of ice water on the lamp stand beside the bed and I held it out to him. He lifted himself up slightly and sipped at it, then fell back against the pillow as if exhausted.

"It was Betty June Lucas's murder you wanted to confess to, wasn't it?" I asked.

He gave a despairing shrug. "I didn't know," he said. "Not until she collapsed. Didn't know who they were for."

"You gave the pills to Dexter?"

He nodded, closing his eyes.

I thought about it. Dexter had seemed to think he had no reason to feel guilty about Betty June's death, and—even given Dexter's skewed notions about guilt and innocence—he'd seemed sincere.

"Did Dexter give the pills to someone else?" I asked.

Blaine opened his eyes and gave me a cloudy, puzzled look, as though he'd forgotten I was there. "I don't know," he said.

"Do you know of anyone who might have wanted her dead?"

He gave a gurgling sigh. "Only Rob," he said.

"Rob? I thought he loved her."

"He did. That's why. Because of Elmore . . ."

"Elmore? You mean Enright? What did he . . . ?"

"They were lovers. Betty June and Elmore. Everyone knew."

I took a second to digest that. "Rob, too?" I asked. I thought of Rob, in his office, reacting to the suggestion that Enright might have been gay, describing his "coarse" sexuality.

"I assume so," Blaine said. "I heard she was planning to leave Rob, go live with Elmore."

Things were clicking into place. First kill the unfaithful wife, then wait a year and kill the lover? Rob had been the one who found the body. Was he that cool and calculating? How different had he been before the guilt and the pills had begun working on him—and how much of that was an act?

"Did he ask you not to do an autopsy on Betty June?" I asked Blaine.

He shook his head. "I knew what I'd find," he said miserably. "I recognized the signs."

I'd been leaning over Blaine, to hear him better. Now I straightened up and stretched my back a bit. His clawlike hand came out from under the covers and clutched at my pants leg.

"What now?" he asked.

I looked down at him a moment before answering. "I'm not sure," I said. "There's still a lot to work out. Captain Mike Farrar will be up to talk to you, and you should tell him everything you've told me, and anything else you know. Is there anything else?"

"The drug company," he said. "The ones who send the stuff for Dexter. They're in Philadelphia."

That part became a bit clearer. It wasn't random samples Blaine had been passing on to Dexter, but prearranged shipments, masquerading as samples. I wondered if Philadelphia was the part of "back east" that Nick was from. There would be money in it somewhere, too. I wondered where Nick was right now, and what he was doing.

"Anything else?" I asked.

"The boy."

"What boy? Eddie Skubitz?"

"He was strangled."

"I know that," I said.

Blaine shook his head with as much force as he was capable of. "Not with his shirt," he said. "He was dead already."

It took me a second to get it, and then I stood in silence, stunned. Who would have wanted Eddie dead? Someone who was afraid of what he might say if he talked, obviously. Which probably meant whoever killed Enright. But who could have gotten to him, in his cell? Someone powerful enough to do that, or to get someone on the force to do it for him. It occurred to me that Bullard, with his bad hand, might be the only one in the clear.

"Why didn't you tell anyone before?" I asked Blaine. And then I realized that he would have drawn the same conclusion I just had, as soon as he examined the body. As far as he'd known, I could have been the killer.

"It's hard to know who to trust," he said.

I nodded. "You got that right, doc," I said.

Back at the station, I went in through the front lobby, not caring much whether anyone saw me or not. But Mike and Bullard were both out. I went across the alley to the jail and checked the visitors' log for Eddie Skubitz the day he'd died.

"Nobody," the jailer said. "Who would there be? It wasn't visiting hours."

"And nobody got in?"

"Nobody who wasn't s'posed to. What do you mean?" His eyes narrowed, as though I were accusing him of something. Maybe I was.

"Some people don't have to follow the formalities," I said. "The mayor, people like that . . ."

He shook his head stubbornly. "Nobody like that," he said. "Nobody."

But of course there had been somebody. The panicky feeling in my gut rose again. I chewed on it all the way back to the police station. As I was going through the lobby, the dispatcher yelled at me.

"Detective Branch. Captain Farrar's been trying to find you."

I stepped in and waited while he made contact.

"This is eleven," Mike's tinny voice said at last.

"Detective Branch is here in the radio room," the dispatcher said.

"Have him stand by," Mike said. "I'll call on a land line."

"10-4."

After a minute the phone rang and the dispatcher handed it to me.

"Johnny?"

"Yeah. Listen, Mike. I talked to Blaine. He didn't kill Dexter, but he confirmed that it was the cyanide that killed Betty June. Also . . ."

"Johnny," he said again.

"What?"

"Jesus, Johnny, I'm sorry to be the one."

"What?"

"It's Marcie Skubitz. She's been murdered. Just like Dexter, two in the back of the head."

I stood in silence, holding the phone. The dispatcher gave me a funny look. No, I thought, that's a mistake. It doesn't make any sense. There's been some mistake.

"Johnny?" Mike said from far away.

"Yeah," I said.

"You okay?"

"Yeah," I said. But I wasn't. My whole body felt numb, the way your elbow does at first, when you bang it against something, just before the pain starts. And I knew the pain was coming, and with it something else: the old panic and the old anger. It can be such a pleasure to ride that anger sometimes, to just go with it. I remembered. The dispatcher reached over and took the phone from my hand, and I saw that my hand was trembling. I could hear Mike's tiny voice calling my name, from far away, and then the dispatcher said something to him, but I wasn't listening. Someone's made a bad mistake this time, I was thinking.

CHAPTER
FIFTEEN

Two miles out of town, the old highway crossed a little creek, and on the other side there was a dirt road that ran along beside it, the creek hidden from the road by cottonwoods and thick underbrush. There were official vehicles scattered all along the dirt road—a couple of sheriff's cars, a highway patrol car, Mike's unmarked car, a yellow emergency vehicle—and half a dozen uniformed men wandered in the roadway and on both sides of it, scanning the ground.

A highway patrolman glanced up at me, recognized me, and pointed off to the side. "Down there," he said. There was a sort of path between a couple of the trees, leading at an angle down the steep, short bank. At the bottom was a little shelf of land sticking out from the bank, and Marcie lay on it, facedown. She was dressed, but her clothes all seemed to have been pulled loose, unbuttoned and unzipped. Her panties were twisted around her ankles. Jack Molini was kneeling on the ground, picking up something. Mike Farrar stood talking with a couple of other officers. He glanced up at me as I approached, then did a double take and came toward me.

"I told you I'd come talk to you," he said accusingly.

"I had to see," I said. I went past him and stood beside Molini.

"What you got?" I asked him.

"Her purse," he said without looking up. "It was open. Contents scattered all over."

"Robbery?"

He stood up, dusting off his trouser legs, and shrugged. "Either that or someone tried to make it look that way," he said.

I nodded.

"Someone tried to make it look like sexual assault, too," he said, "but it's not convincing. The clothes are all loosened, pulled apart. But nothing's really off. Nothing's torn. Her bra's undisturbed. Why would a rapist undo all her clothes but not take them off, and not even unfasten her bra? And there's no sign of a struggle. It looks more like an execution. I'll know more later, but right now I'd say she was killed before her clothing was undone, and I don't think we'll find any evidence of rape."

I finally looked at the body, seeing what Molini was talking about. She lay on her stomach, her arms at her sides, her legs slightly bent, as though she'd gone to her knees first, then fallen over—on her knees when she'd been shot, probably. I'd seen killings like that before, had listened to the killers later describing the victim's pleas for life, knowing the bullet was coming at any second. I blocked the image that was forming in my mind of Marcie in that position, and forced myself to focus on the details in front of me. Her blouse was flared out on either side, and pulled up, exposing her bare back. Her blond hair was tied up in a bun, the way she did when she was doing housework or yard work, and, apart from the bullet hole just behind one ear, it didn't even seem mussed. I'm not an expert on sexual crimes, but I know you don't see too many victims whose hair doesn't get mussed.

"What was in the purse?" I asked, making myself follow the script.

Molini shrugged. "The usual stuff." He'd spread it out on

a plastic sheet beside the body. There were three lipsticks in different shades, a little plastic compact, a half roll of clove Lifesavers, a plastic cardholder with her driver's license and Social Security card and some photos, a folded page torn from the phone book, a library card, a thin wallet with some cash in it, what looked like several ancient grocery lists, a fair quantity of lipstick-stained tissue, a vitamin C bottle with two tablets rattling inside, and some unrecognizable lint and fluff. The photos included a recent one of her brother; one of the two of them, as children, beneath the tree in their backyard; several of older people I didn't recognize— probably their parents and other relatives—and none of me. No reason there should have been. It was stupid, but it hurt a little that you couldn't tell she'd ever known me.

"No checkbook or credit cards," I said.

"No, but she might not have been carrying them. Why take those and not take the cash in the wallet?"

I nodded. The gold compact she'd retrieved at Enright's place wasn't there either. I lifted the torn telephone book page carefully and unfolded it. It was from the yellow pages, but nothing was circled or underlined. One side of the page was all insurance companies, and the other ran from "Interior Decorators" to "Laundries–Self Service," with everything in the *J*'s and *K*'s in between.

I looked down at the body again, trying now to see how this killing might fit in with the others, but I found myself resisting that. I didn't care about the others anymore—just this one. I hadn't been thinking about Marcie much the last couple of days, involved with Clarice and her brother, but now I realized that it hadn't been over between us. Maybe we wouldn't have gotten back together, or maybe if we had it would have ended badly. Still . . . it hadn't been over; there had been more to come, good or bad. And now someone had taken that away, and I wanted whoever that was. I wanted to see him dead, the way I'd seen Doolie Waters dead. I knew it was the same feeling, and I didn't care. It wasn't how a

163

cop was supposed to think, but I didn't care about that anymore either.

"I'm sorry, Johnny," someone said, and I found Bullard standing beside me. Mike was right behind him, looking away from both of us, seeming sad and embarrassed.

I nodded, refolded the phone book page, and handed it back to Molini.

"Mike told me about the cyanide," Bullard said. "We're opening a file on Betty June Lucas. Looks like you were right, about there being something else going on here. You ready to come back to work?"

I looked at him. "You knew about Dexter and the drugs," I said.

Bullard gave a sigh and looked off toward the tops of the trees along the creek. Molini gave us a glance and moved off up the path, carrying his bundle of evidence. "Bunch of rich people gettin' their jollies at parties," Bullard said. "Who could give a shit? We both saw worse stuff than that in Kansas City, happening right out on the street. They weren't hurting anyone else, that I could see. Hell, I'm not sure there was anything really illegal going on."

"I heard Dexter's speech," I told him. "The thing is, you didn't try very hard to find out." Bullard started to say something, but I waved a hand at him. "Fuck that," I said. "I know what you're saying. I don't care about it, either. What I care about is Eddie and Marcie. They didn't have any business getting in the middle of this and getting themselves killed."

"Eddie killed himself," Bullard said.

I studied him for a moment. He looked like he believed it.

"You need to talk to Dr. Blaine," I said. "He'll tell you some things you don't know—about where the drugs came from. And how Eddie died." I saw Mike's head come up sharply. I turned away from the two of them and started walking back up the path to the road.

"Johnny," Mike said, his voice sounding choked.

"Wait," Bullard said to me, cutting him off. "We need to talk about it, coordinate the investigation."

I stopped and looked back at him. "You coordinate the investigation," I said. "You and Mike. I'm not a cop anymore."

"You're pissed," Bullard said. "I understand that. But I didn't kill her, and neither did Mike, and there's no reason to burn all your bridges right now. I made a mistake. I admit it. I'm sorry."

"You didn't make a mistake," I said. "I should have figured out in Kansas City that I was in the wrong line of work. I'm no good at it, not when it counts. If I were, Marcie wouldn't be dead now."

"You can't blame yourself for these things," Bullard said. "Cops can't think that way."

"I know," I said. "That's exactly what I mean." I turned away again.

"You've gotta be with us on this or keep out of it," Bullard called after me. "Otherwise, you're against us."

I glanced back once more, saw Mike's pale face behind Bullard's shoulder, but didn't say anything. We looked into one another's eyes for a second and then I turned again and went up the path to my car.

Marcie hadn't had much, but what she'd had was strewn all over the house. All the drawers in the little bureau in the living room had been pulled out and dumped on the faded rug. There were old family photo albums, a couple of tablecloths, a lot of little knickknacks—souvenirs of family trips to the Ozarks and Worlds of Fun. The little drawer in the end table beside the sofa lay upside down on the floor, and Marcie's sewing stuff—her spools of thread, her pin cushion, the flimsy patterns she'd bought in packets at K mart—were heaped beside it. The sofa cushions had been thrown out into the middle of the floor and someone had pulled the lint and the old ballpoints and all the other effluvia out from the sofa linings. I saw a plastic child's block, a food-encrusted spoon, some greenish pennies.

The bedroom was much the same—just worse, because there was more there to go through. It was all sad and pathetic and I felt my anger growing as I went through the house, yet at the same time I felt cold and clearheaded, as though the anger were somehow separate from me, a resource I could call on whenever I needed it. The more the better.

The house didn't tell me much. The fact that the search was so thorough indicated that whoever it was hadn't found what he was looking for, unless it was in the very last place he looked. The only things I could think of that he might have been looking for were the compact—which I didn't find anywhere—and the money. I doubted that the money had ever been here, but the killer might have thought it was. It seemed to me the money was the thing that was throwing everyone off—me, Bullard, the killer, maybe even Marcie and Eddie—making us all make mistakes that couldn't be undone.

The kitchen was a nightmare of spilled foods and pots and pans and silverware, the refrigerator door hanging open. I stepped through it and went down the back steps. The yard had been mowed since the day I'd told Marcie about Eddie's death, and it looked empty and naked—just the big old elm and the rusting shed at the rear corner, the empty clothesline along the back. I went to the shed and looked in. It, too, had been gone through. There were plastic and metal jugs thrown here and there, a strong odor of insecticide mixed with gasoline.

Going back to the house, I stopped and looked at the big old tree, remembering the photo from Marcie's purse, of her and Eddie. In that photo, there'd been a tire swing dangling behind them, and I could see where one of the branches still bore the mark of the rope. Farther up, there was a remnant of thin planking hanging from a nail—all that was left of the tree house their father had built.

I walked around to the other side of the tree, the side facing the next-door yard, and found the hollow where Marcie and Eddie, as children, had hidden their most secret things, their most treasured possessions, the things the grownups might take away from them. I put my hand inside. The gold compact was nestled in its bottom, wrapped neatly in tissue paper.

I stood for a moment, holding it, feeling my heart pound in my throat. Probably she'd just put it there because it was a favorite hiding place, but it was possible she'd thought of me when she did it, known it was a place I might think to look. Finally, I opened the compact, but there was nothing inside. I bounced it in my hand, studying it, trying to understand what its importance was. It seemed strange to me now that I'd thought it was the kind of thing Enright might have given Marcie, the kind of thing a man like him might give to a truck stop waitress. It was more the kind of thing a man like him might give to someone like Betty June Lucas.

I went back into the house and looked for the phone. The little metal table where it normally sat was on its side and the phone was nowhere in sight, but I followed the cord from the wall through the heap of clutter and found it lying under one of the sofa cushions, beeping softly to itself. It was the phone book I wanted, and that lay beside it, the pages splayed out. I riffled through it to the place where Marcie had torn out the page, and tried to remember everything that had been on that page, but I couldn't come up with anything.

I went out and got in my car and drove to a gas station that had a public phone. I ran my eye down the listings on the page, and stopped at "Jewelers." Chewing at my lower lip, I dialed the first of the three numbers.

"This is Detective Branch with the Elk Rapids Police Department," I lied. "I'm enquiring about a gold-plated compact. We have reason to believe that a young woman may have brought one in recently. . . ."

"Oh, yes," the man said. "But it was gold, not gold-plated. Very nice. She wanted to know if we'd sold it."

"And had you?"

"No. Not one of ours."

The second number was pay dirt.

"Yes," the woman said. "The young lady said she'd found it and wanted to return it if she could determine the owner. Unusual to find that kind of honesty these days. It had no engraving, no identifying marks. She could easily have just kept it. Or simply put an ad in the paper, for that matter. I hope she's not in any trouble. I was impressed with her sense of duty. She was very serious about it."

"No," I said. "She's not in any trouble now. Were you able to help her?"

"Oh, yes. It was one we'd special-ordered about two years ago. A birthday gift."

"For whom?"

"Well, I wouldn't know for whom. I only know who bought it. Mr. Lucas, at the newspaper. I assume it was for his wife. You know she died soon after that. So sudden. Very tragic. Perhaps he didn't really want it anymore, after she died, and that's how it ended up with the young lady."

"Perhaps," I said.

Before I got back in my car, I dialed the police station and left a message for Bullard.

CHAPTER
SIXTEEN

Evening was settling in on Circle Street. A breeze blew leaves across the big neat lawns, and here and there someone sat in a porch swing reading the paper, a father tossed a ball to a small boy who put both hands in front of his face and missed it, a slightly overweight Irish setter padded happily beside a young girl who jogged along the curving sidewalk, her yellow headband wrapped around her earphones. The smell of barbecue drifted in the air.

Clarice answered the doorbell, wearing white tennis shorts and a blue sleeveless terry-cloth shirt. She started to smile when she saw me, but then her smiled faded.

"What is it?" she asked.

"Rob," I said.

She studied me for a moment, then said, "He's upstairs. I'll get him."

When she'd gone, I went into the living room. If someone tore everything apart here and scattered it around on the floor, it would make a much bigger pile, I thought. Much more impressive, too. There probably weren't any old ballpoint pens lost in the linings of the big white sofa. Maybe a swizzle stick or two. Maybe some designer drugs.

Rob came down looking a lot more chipper than he had outside Dexter's office that morning. Why not? Most of the people who could link him to Betty June's death were out of the way now. He wore beige slacks and a white polo shirt that set off his tan.

"More questions?" he asked. He waved toward the armchair, but I ignored the invitation. He shrugged and sat down there himself, crossing his legs. Clarice came into the room, looking uneasy, and sat down on the end of the sofa nearest to Rob. She'd put on a baggy, unzipped sweatshirt and had her hands deep in the pockets, as if she were cold.

I took the compact out of my jacket pocket and showed it to Rob. "Recognize this?" I asked.

His eyes widened a bit and he glanced at Clarice, then back at me. "Why, yes," he said. "Where did you get it?"

"Marcie Skubitz had it," I said. "I think she was trying to find out who it belonged to because she thought it had something to do with Walter Enright getting killed, and that it might help clear her brother."

Rob stared at me blankly, glancing at his sister again, as if for help, then shook his head and said, "I don't understand."

"I think you do," I said. "I'm pretty sure this is what you were after when you tore up the Skubitz place, because this is what connects Betty June to Walter Enright."

"Betty June? What . . ."

"I think Marcie traced it to you finally, and then confronted you with it, and you killed her."

Lucas started to make some protest. He looked more hurt than angry.

"Rob," Clarice said, cutting him off. "You don't have to say anything. I'll call Burt Condon." She stood up, glaring at me, but didn't actually move toward the phone.

Lucas licked his lips. "Are you arresting me?" he asked.

"Not me," I said. "I'm not a cop anymore."

He looked puzzled for a second, then gave an odd, forced smile, an echo of the kind I'd seen him give during televised interviews and debates, when someone scored a point or asked a tough question. "Look now . . ." he began.

"You shouldn't have killed her," I said. "That was your mistake. That made it personal."

His smile faded. "You're crazy," he said. "You can't threaten me. You don't even know what you're talking about. That isn't even Betty June's compact. It never was. It's . . ."

"It's mine," Clarice said. She'd taken the little jeweled gun out of her sweatshirt pocket and was pointing it at my stomach. "I've been looking for it. Just put it on the sofa right there."

"Clarice, what are you . . . ?" Rob began, but she gave him a quick sidelong glance that shut him up. "Is everybody crazy?" he asked no one in particular.

I stared at her for a moment, then tossed the compact onto the sofa. I was ready to go for my gun when she made a grab at it, but she didn't. She kept her eyes and her gun on me, a little smile on her lips.

"You really thought Rob could kill someone?" she asked. "Don't you know I'm the one who does the hard things?"

Rob was staring at her, his mouth partway open.

"Starting with Betty June," I said.

Clarice shrugged. "Something had to be done," she said. "Rob had no willpower where she was concerned. He would have let her destroy us. Everything we'd worked for."

"Clare," Rob said in a reproachful whisper.

She glanced at him and her face softened momentarily, but her eyes slid quickly back to me. "She was going to go off with him. Elmore. Enright. Whatever his name was. She was just going to move in over there, two doors away. Can you imagine what a laughingstock Rob would have been? He would have been a joke. Nobody would have voted for him. We'd worked too hard to let that little cunt ruin everything."

"It was you making sure Rob got the pills," I said. "Dexter was just helping you."

"It was the easiest way. We didn't have time for therapy.

171

He had to get through it, go on with things." She made a face. "It just got out of hand," she said. Her eyes turned cold. "If you hadn't gotten involved . . ."

"What about Enright?" I asked. "Did something get out of hand there, too?" I gave Rob a quick glance, to see how he was taking all this. He was slumped far forward, his hands hanging between his legs, a fixed look of pain on his face. I wondered if he was getting one of his headaches.

Clarice pursed her lips. "Betty June had told him some things," she said. "About the drugs and some other things—things that could embarrass us. And he was suspicious about her death." She shrugged. "But he was easy to handle. He was a classic case of the older male, feeling himself growing impotent, trying to reassert himself. First, with the boy, shaping him, controlling his life, and then with Betty June, and then . . ." She paused and gave an ugly little smile. "Not that he was impotent, literally. But it wasn't really sex with him; it was power. He didn't really understand that, but I did. It was making people do things that he liked, especially things they didn't like to do—especially young, attractive women. That was why he liked me better than Betty June. She was just a stupid slut who liked being dominated, but I knew what he was after, and I was willing to pretend to be disgusted by his demands. He couldn't get enough of that." She laughed at the expression on my face. "Men have these fantasies they think are so shocking," she said, "and it's really all so pathetic and predictable. It's like pushing buttons."

"Even with Dexter," I said.

"Especially Dexter. He was in love with me. He was the easiest of all." She gave another harsh laugh.

"And Rob," I said.

She stopped smiling. "Don't misunderstand me," she said. "Everything I did was for Rob." She glanced at him, but the expression on his face must have startled her, for she looked quickly back at me. "You're stalling," she said. "I

172

understand that. But it doesn't matter. Everything's under control.''

"You said that about Enright," I said. "If it was so, why kill him?''

She shrugged. "It was an accident, really. Eddie was keeping an eye on him for me. . . .''

"Eddie?" I said.

"He knew there was something going on between Bill and me, and he was jealous. He'd do anything I asked." She paused. "He never asked anything of me, never made any demands—the only one who didn't,'' she said, then shook her head slightly. "I really was sorry to see him in jail, but there wasn't anything I could do about it. Maybe his suicide was the best thing.'' She paused again, seeming to have lost her train of thought. After a moment, her expression cleared and she said, "Eddie told me there was something buried in the garden and something hidden behind the furnace. I don't think he knew what either thing was. He never said, anyway. He just gave me the map. If I'd known what it was, I would have handled it differently. I just wanted some leverage to offset the leverage Bill had over us, but when I hinted that I knew something, he went wild. He tried to strangle me. I fell over the coffee table and turned my ankle, trying to get away, and Eddie came in and jumped him, trying to help me, and I managed to get hold of the candy dish and I hit him with it. It was really self-defense.''

"Except that the first blow didn't kill him," I said.

She shrugged. "That's true. We thought he was dead, and we began going around straightening things up, trying to hide what had happened, and he came to and tried to get up, and I hit him again—a couple of times, I guess—and then he really was dead. I was just wearing my bathrobe, and I was panicky. Eddie told me to go on and he'd take care of everything. I guess he found the compact and the map and took it with him. When he was arrested, I thought he'd talk, but he didn't. He was willing to die for me." Her eyes glistened with tears. I felt moved and disgusted by her at the same time.

"What about the money in Enright's basement?" I asked.

She looked at me, blinking, seeming to come back to the present. "I don't know," she said offhandedly. "I assumed Eddie took it, until his sister showed up that night. Maybe Dexter knew about it." She shrugged, dismissing it.

"Clare," Rob said in a husky voice. "You really killed Betty June?" His face had relaxed some, but he looked about twenty years older than he had a half hour before.

Clarice looked sidelong at him, keeping an eye on me. "We'll talk about it later, baby," she said. "She wasn't a good person. She was going to hurt you."

"So what now?" I asked.

"So now . . ." she began, but then Rob made a lunge at her, going for the gun. She saw him out of the corner of her eye and swung the gun quickly, instinctively, chopping him hard on the side of the head. He went down in a heap at her feet, blood oozing from a cut. I had my hand on my gun butt, under the jacket, but she had me covered again before I could get it out. He eyes were still glistening, but were now bright with anger.

"That's your fault," she said. "It's because of you I had to hurt him. Now I'll take . . ."

The doorbell rang and we both froze, staring at one another. In the silence, Rob gave a heavy grunt, like a sleeper disturbed.

"That'll be the police," I said, hoping it was so. "I left a message for Chief Bullard, telling him I was coming here to arrest Rob."

Her face remained calm as she considered that. "Doesn't matter," she said at last. "I've got you. You'll get me out of here. Show me the gun."

I pulled back the left wing of my jacket, revealing the .357 in its holster, beneath my left arm.

"Use your left hand," she said. "Pull it out with two fingers and toss it on the couch beside the compact."

It was awkward, but I managed. She kept her gaze level on me all the time, despite the doorbell ringing again. When I'd tossed the gun, she stepped sideways toward it, picked it up, and put her own little gun back in her sweatshirt pocket. She cocked the .357, chambering a slug.

"Turn around," she said.

We both heard the front door open, and then Mike Farrar's voice calling, "Johnny?"

I was about to shout a warning, but Clarice called out, "Stay where you are." Her voice was surprisingly sharp and clear, the kind of voice people were likely to obey. "Turn around," she said to me again, hissing.

I did. She came up close behind me and pressed the barrel firmly into my ribs. "I imagine this makes a pretty big hole in a person," she said. "You saw how quick I am a moment ago, and you know I won't hesitate to shoot."

"You're going to have to kill me," I said. "Otherwise I'm going to kill you."

"Because of the girl, you mean." I could imagine the half smile on her face. "Okay. Whatever you say. But first we get out of this."

"There's no way you're going to get out of this," I said.

"We'll see."

"What about Rob?"

"The best thing I can do for him now is disappear. It's what I was planning to do, anyway, if Eddie talked. I've got it all planned. Every contingency is covered. Rob still has time to dissociate himself politically from his crazy sister. He knew nothing. He's innocent."

"He may not think so," I said. "Being ignorant may not be all he needs to feel innocent."

She jabbed me hard in the kidneys with the gun barrel. "You don't care about Rob," she said. "You're just stalling. Let's go."

I walked out of the living room and into the entrance foyer. Mike was standing in the open doorway. I expected him to have his gun out, but he didn't.

"Take your gun out and throw it down," Clarice said to him.

Mike didn't seem to hear what she said. He wasn't even looking at her. He just stood where he was, blocking the door, looking at me.

"Don't be foolish, Mike," I said. "She'll kill you. She killed the others."

"I'm sorry, Johnny," Mike said to me, still oblivious to Clarice. "I know you talked to the jailer, and I intercepted your message to Bullard. I had to straighten it out with you first."

I'd been counting on some uniforms outside. I wondered if Clarice understood, from what he'd just said, that there weren't any.

"Get out of the way," she said to him calmly. "If you don't, I'll shoot you."

Mike shook his head sadly. I couldn't tell if it was a response to what she had said.

"Mike," I said.

"It was so much money," he said. "And nobody knew about it. And it didn't really belong to anyone. I thought it might as well belong to Eleanor and me, that's all. I thought we deserved something like that. I never meant to hurt anyone. I want you to believe that."

"I believe it," I said.

"I'm going to shoot you," Clarice said. "That's what you'd better believe." Her voice had grown a bit shrill. She didn't know what was going on between Mike and me, couldn't figure out why he seemed to be ignoring her, and it threw her. It was a contingency she didn't have covered. The pressure of the gun barrel on my ribs went away, and I knew she was taking a step backward, to get an angle on both of us. I was thinking that if I had some way of knowing when she went for Mike, I could get an elbow into her gut.

"Mike," I said. "She'll kill you."

"It was for Eleanor," he said, and I saw that there were tears in his eyes. "The kid started talking and I panicked. Because it was all so complicated all of a sudden. Once he started talking, it wasn't going to be simple anymore. And he knew about the money, so everyone would know. If it had just been me . . ." He shook his head, giving me a look of utter sadness. "But I had to do it, for Eleanor. I couldn't see any other way. I just wanted him to shut up, that's all."

"I just want you to shut up, goddamn you," Clarice said.

He looked at her for the first time. "I knew it was you all along," he said casually. "The kid told me. I was going to let you get away with it, so I could get away. But I can't. Somebody has to pay."

"Move, goddamn you," Clarice hissed.

He did. He began walking toward her.

"Mike," I said, feeling desperate. He wasn't going for his gun. He was just walking toward us with his hands down at his side, like someone's grampa arriving for Sunday dinner.

It seemed to confuse Clarice. She'd shot a couple of people in cold blood, but maybe not when they were facing her like this.

"Stop," she said, her voice cracking slightly. She sounded afraid for the first time. Mike just kept coming, saying something under his breath that I couldn't hear. I swallowed and began to dip my shoulder and pivot, hoping I could catch her looking at him.

I wasn't quick enough. She fired just as I began to move, the bullet catching Mike in the right side of his chest and spinning him slightly. I drove toward Clarice like a defensive lineman, staying low, keeping my legs under me, expecting the punch of the bullet in my shoulder or head. Instead, she tried to sidestep, and I caught her hip with my shoulder,

177

sending her flying. I ended up beyond her, on my knees. When I looked up, she had a hand against the wall, getting her balance. She still held my gun and it was still pointing at me.

"I'd kill you right now," she said, breathing heavily, "but I'm not sure there aren't some more cops out there, and I still need you to get out. We'll go out the back way." She made a little pointing motion with the barrel, toward the living room.

I glanced at Mike's body, which lay motionless, then got up and walked that way. Back in the living room, Rob was on his knees in front of the white sofa, which was stained with his blood. He had both hands pressed against his temples and there was dried blood on the fingers of his left hand.

He looked up at me as I came in, his eyes squinting as though he were looking into a bright light.

"My head," he said. "Oh, god. My head."

"Help him," Clarice said. Her voice was a strangled whisper. "His pills."

"Where are they?" I asked.

Her eyes darted back and forth for a moment, as though she expected to spot them somewhere in the living room. She put a hand to her own head, perhaps in sympathetic pain.

"His bedroom," she said distractedly. I could see the wheels spinning behind her eyes, as she tried to figure out how to get the pills and keep me under control. "Help him up," she said at last. "You'll help him upstairs. Carry him if you have to."

I stepped closer to Rob and knelt beside him. "Can you get up?" I asked him.

He gave me a dazed look, like someone who's not quite sure where he is. After a second, he held out a hand to me and I took it. I stood up and put my other hand under his arm to help him to his feet. Clarice was standing near the door to the hallway, her eyes wide, chewing unconsciously on her lower lip.

As Rob climbed to his feet, leaning against me to get his balance, Nick Adrian materialized in the archway just behind Clarice. Maybe she heard him, or maybe she saw something in my eyes, because she began to pivot that way, swinging the gun barrel. She wasn't quick enough. The knife blade came up gleaming in front of her eyes, and Nick had his other hand on the wrist that held the gun.

"Stay still," he said softly, perhaps talking to all of us. "Throw the gun. I want to hear it hit the wall."

Clarice hesitated a moment, staring at me, her jaw working as though she were chewing on something, and then she tossed the .357 sideways. It bounced on the floor just below the curtained window, hit the base of the wall, and slid behind the sofa.

"Good," Nick said. "Now move on into the room."

She took a couple of halting steps forward, looking dazed. Nick stayed about a step behind her. The knife was out of sight now, and I guessed he was holding it against her back.

"Which one of them killed Dexter?" he asked me.

I hesitated. Clarice looked at me with round eyes, but there was no plea for help in them. It was like the look a frightened animal gives you, torn between fighting and fleeing.

"It was her," I said. Beside me, Rob gave a moan of pain. "She killed all of them," I said.

"I don't care about the others," Nick said. "Dexter was my responsibility. I screwed up. I have to do something about it."

Just like Mike, I thought crazily. "She'll go to jail," I told him, knowing it would make no difference.

Nick gave me a pleasant smile, as if acknowledging a joke. He gave her a shove in the middle of the back and she stumbled toward me. I put out a hand to catch her, but she spun away, falling toward the sofa as she clutched with one hand at the pocket of her sweatshirt.

"Nick," I said. "Look out. She's got . . ."

She was too quick for me, but not quick enough for him. The little designer gun was only halfway out of her pocket when he fired twice, the gun appearing magically in his left hand. Her body jerked backward slightly and then she fell over the arm of the sofa, her hands hanging down. The little gun dropped to the floor.

"I prefer the knife," Nick said. "But I'm not stupid."

Rob had slumped back to the floor, clutching his head. He began crying raggedly, in loud sobs.

Oblivious, Nick took out a handkerchief and began wiping the gun off. He gave me a speculative look. "This belonged to the dead guy out in the hall," he said. "I guess he was a friend of yours. I'm sorry." He set it down carefully on the end table, and we stood looking at each other. All three guns were out of my reach and he still had the knife. I wasn't sure what I wanted to do anyway.

"I can't figure out who owes who, between us," he said. "I think I saved your life just now, and I'll save it again by walking out of here." He smiled. "But that doesn't count," he said. "I wouldn't kill you anyway, unless you made me. You know that, don't you?"

I nodded.

"I'm on my own time now," he said. "That finishes my work here." He nodded toward Clarice's body. "I'll have some explaining to do, but at least I squared things."

I looked where he was looking. Clarice looked like someone who had leaned over the arm of the sofa to pick up something and had then passed out. Her legs still looked slim and strong and attractive beneath the tennis shorts, but they were just so much cold matter now, already on their way to becoming dust. I thought then of Marcie's body on the creek bank, the shambles of her house on the other side of Randall Drive. Things were still relatively neat here on Circle Street, except for the scattered guns and the bloodstains that no one would ever get out of the white sofa. I had a quick, visceral memory of living female flesh against my own, Marcie and

Clarice, and maybe Terry as well, the heat and the softness of life, the things you think you can believe in the dark. When I looked back at Nick, he was gone.

I stood there for a long time. After a while, I took my own handkerchief out and picked up Mike's gun and took it out to the hallway and put it beside his dead hand. Then I took Clarice's little gun from beneath her hand and put it back in her sweatshirt, replacing it with my own gun. The scene wasn't going to make complete sense to Molini, especially the location of the bodies, but I figured, with my statement and Bullard's backing, he wouldn't worry too much about it. After all, he'd spent his whole life in Elk Rapids. He knew how things worked.

CHAPTER
SEVENTEEN

I visited Marcie one last time on my way out of town. I knew she wouldn't like the way things had come out, the parts that had had to be covered up, the deals that had had to be made. I hadn't liked some of it myself, but I'd done the best I could. I just wanted to tell her that.

Of course, the others were there, too—most of them. Eddie was right beside Marcie and their parents, all their names on a single narrow stone. And Mike wasn't far away, back in the old neighborhood, but with a slightly larger stone than the rest, thanks to the unusually large death benefit his widow had gotten from the Police Benevolent Association. That had been part of the deal I'd made with Bullard. I'd found the money in an old washing machine in Mike's garage. The FBI had gotten about half of it back, and they'd decided to be satisfied with that, as well as the story that it had been found in Dexter's apartment.

Dexter was over on the other side of the cemetery, of course, in the better neighborhood, among the big trees and the ornate family stones with their towering crosses and carved angels holding open books in which the important names were graven. Betty June Lucas was there, too, lying beside her in-laws, with Clarice Lucas a short distance away, just enough space between the two of them for Rob, which I suppose was fitting, though I wondered if Rob, at the grave-side ceremony, had thought about lying between the two of them for eternity. I wondered if it had given him a headache.

The only ones missing were Enright and Dixon—but then they'd been outsiders, anyway, like me. They'd been shipped back east for their relatives to dispose of. Wherever they were, I supposed, they were in the good part of the cemetery, the better side of the graveyard. I doubted that they appreci-ated it, though; my guess was they would have all preferred Randall Drive to this neighborhood.

"I thought I might find you here," someone said. I looked around to see Bullard standing behind me.

Neither one of us said anything for a while. We just stood there looking at all the fresh graves. I'd gotten over blaming him for how many there were; I knew he didn't like it any better than I did, that he'd tried to do the right thing all along.

"Still going?" he asked, as we walked together back to-ward where our cars were parked.

I nodded. "Got my stuff in the car. This was my last stop."

"Where to?"

"Don't know, exactly. Back to K.C. for a while, to visit the family. Then I'll decide."

"I know you hate it right now," he said, "but maybe police work is what you ought to decide on. You really are good at it."

"I don't hate it," I said. "The problem is, I'm only good at parts of it, and the parts I'm not good at are the parts that get people killed. That's what I hate."

He shrugged. We'd had this discussion already; neither one of us had anything new to say. "Things are going to be different around here," he said. "You know that."

I looked at him for a moment, then nodded. "But there'll be another Dexter," I said. "There always is."

He nodded. "I know," he said. "But I'll know how to handle it this time. I know what I'm doing."

"Perspective," I said.

He pursed his lips, not quite a smile.

"Just remember," he said. "When it came down to it, I was on your side."

I nodded. "But was that the right side?" I asked, then waved off his response. "I know you'll do a good job here, Pat," I said. "I just can't be a part of it."

We stopped between our cars and shook hands. Then he went and got in and drove off, the white dust of the cemetery spiraling in the air behind him, making a kind of wall between the one side and the other, glistening like something solid in the shafts of morning sunlight, hiding Bullard's car finally and the way he had gone, the high road back to the neighborhoods of the living.

On the front seat in my own car were some loose things I'd collected at the last minute, clearing out my apartment, including the unsigned letter I'd received in that day's mail. It was just a sheet of cream-colored paper in a matching envelope, with my name and address in a neat, spidery hand and no return address, postmarked Philadelphia. What the letter said was: "Don't forget that drink. Anytime." That was followed only by a phone number with a 215 area code.

I picked it up for a moment and looked at it, then shook my head and laughed and tossed it back on top of the other odds and ends left over from my life in Elk Rapids. But once I started laughing, I had trouble stopping for a while, and when I did the laughter left moisture in the corners of my eyes. I remembered Clarice laughing, the night we'd come back from Independence and made love on the white sofa. I remembered Terry Gardens laughing in her apartment in Old Westport above the coffeehouse, the Picasso prints on the walls and the secondhand bookstores across the street, where we'd pulled down dusty books with odd titles, daring each to guess what they'd be about. The only one whose laughter I couldn't remember was Marcie—when I thought of her I still saw only the sadness and the pity on her face when she'd told me I was no use to her, the pain on her face in the interrogation room at the station, when she'd told me the gold compact was hers and then waited to see whether I'd believe it or not, and thinking of her in those ways still caused a tearing pain down inside me, a pain I suspected I'd never quite be free of.

But did it really mean you couldn't trust the laughter, only the sadness and the pain? That's how it had seemed to me in the days after the final scene on Circle Street, getting things sorted out, finding answers for the FBI and the district attorney, easing Rob out of the campaign and into drug therapy as quietly as possible, getting Eleanor Farrar settled in her new nursing home, persuading Blaine to retire and keep his mouth shut—just generally helping Bullard tie up the loose ends and keep Elk Rapids from finding out too much about the rot that had been cut out of it. But now, driving out of the cemetery, turning away from Elk Rapids, toward the open country and the highway north, it seemed to me that I was taking a first step toward a place where none of that would be necessary anymore, where it might be possible again to trust the good things, if I could only find my way back.

ABOUT THE AUTHOR

Jeffrey Tharp lives in a small town in south-central Kansas.